Gajapati Kapilendra Deva

&

His Mastodon Power

Gajapati Kapilendra Deva
&
His Mastodon Power

Indramani Jena

BLACK EAGLE BOOKS
Dublin, USA | Bhubaneswar, India

Black Eagle Books
USA address:
7464 Wisdom Lane
Dublin, OH 43016

India address:
E/312, Trident Galaxy, Kalinga Nagar,
Bhubaneswar-751003, Odisha, India

E-mail: info@blackeaglebooks.org
Website: www.blackeaglebooks.org

First International Edition Published by
Black Eagle Books, 2023

GAJAPATI KAPILENDRA DEVA & HIS MASTODON POWER
by **Indramani Jena**

Copyright © Indramani Jena

Cover & Interior Design: Ezy's Publication

ISBN- 978-1-64560-483-9 (Paperback)
Library of Congress Control Number: 2023951124

Printed in the United States of America

A Tribute to Gajapati Kapilendra Deva

The author dedicates the book to the indomitable Gajapati Kapilendra Deva, a paragon of bravery and resilience, who boldly proclaimed, "Odisha is our kingdom, Odia is our state language, and Lord Jagannath is our state deity." He stood as a formidable presence on the battlefield, a fearless Hindu king during the fifteenth century in the vast land of Bharatavarsha. His valour and unwavering spirit have left an enduring legacy in the annals of history.

Significance of Vijaya Bahuda in life of Gajapati Kapilendra Deva

During the reign of Gajapati Kapilendra Deva, the Odia term "Vijaya Bahuda" was there since Kalinga, the erstwhile Odisha's win over the Satavahana. This term symbolised a victorious march back to the capital after conquering territories in the South. Kapilendra Deva, known for his military prowess, assigned the governance of the captured lands to *Parichhas* and then proudly returned to his capital, Bidanasi Cuttack, under the triumphant banner of victory.

Interestingly, the name "Vijayawada" today is believed to have evolved from "Vijaya Bahuda." This city, situated on the north bank of the sacred river Krishna, was once part of the *Vamsakundin* kingdom, allies of Jeypore Empire dynasty of Koraput.

In the cluster of villages known as Bhurimi, located in the western mountain range, Gajapati Kapilendra constructed a castle. During his reign, the temples in the region were under the care of priest-cum-Brahmins, emphasizing the rich cultural and religious heritage of his rule.

The mention of the Indakuladi hill in the Eastern Ghats is steeped in mythology. It is believed that during the era of the Mahabharata, Arjuna, a descendant of Pandu, acquired the powerful weapon *Pasupat* through intense penance at this very spot. This hill and its surrounding may have been chosen as the final resting place for the devout and holy life of the remarkable Gajapati King, Kapilendra Deva, underscoring his significance in history.

Dr Narayan Sahu
Prof. and Head Bhasa Sahitya Bibhaga
Utkal University, Vani Vihar, Bhubaneswar

Introduction

This earth has mothered the bravest men for ages and seen their heroic charisma. If sometimes their bravery has blazed from somewhere on her bosom, some ineffective kingdoms have warriors shown examples of deft swordsmanship. She is a wonderful lady indeed. In her history, such an event had happened a couple of centuries ago. And it was in the reign of Gajapati, the bravest of the brave, who galvanized the formidable military might for thirty years. The Utkal, which was shrinking fast because neighbouring *Yavana* (Muslim) and Hindu kings nibbled away in parts, again got annexed as a tax-paying principality into the extensive empire of Odisha and its widespread territory. He spent the best of his time in military expeditions, but his contribution to our society, culture, language and literature is estimated to be of the highest order. Many research scholars have rightly called his age the Golden Era of Odisha. During the reign of the Ganga dynasty, the integrity and administration of the kingdom of Odisha were very high. The dynasty ruled from 1075 to 1434 AD. During this period, Ganga kings, fond of temples, built the Jagannath temple at Puri and the Sun temple at Konark. But over time, this family tradition deteriorated. Of course, this is the family history of every dynasty. Narasimha Deva of the Ganga dynasty had an aggressive nature. He was watching intently the Bengal Sultan Ilias Sahi, who was repeatedly plundering the Utkal and Jagannath temple treasuries. Unfortunately, the same Ganga dynasty was under a successor whose time passed only with wine and women. He lost his honourable title 'Gangaraj' for the shameful sobriquet ' *Matta* Bhanudev', which meant 'Mad Bhanudev'. Odisha's borders were porous because of the failure to guard the frontiers at that time and to ensure the kingdom's security. The vigilant courtiers, ministers and servants of Lord Jagannath temple realized that Bhanudev was absent from his capital at Bidanasi Cuttack for months by being engaged in a fruitless fight for long periods with Birabhadra Reddy, who had forcibly annexed the whole tract of Odisha from Rajamahendry to Seemachal or Simadri into his kingdom. At that time, Odisha would be the victim of invasions by the Nawab of Bengal and Sarki Sultan of Jaunpur. The chief interest of all those foreign invaders was the kingdom of Odisha in general and the gems- and jewellery-filled vaults of the Jagannath temple and the highly skilled elephantry of Utkal in particular.

The whole kingdom desperately needed a brave ruler, a consummate military organizer and an astute administrator. Many of those loyalists of the empire who were involved in its administration, too, felt the urgency of a change of guard. Most certainly, in the Odia army, they found an officer endowed with all the virtues of a true leader and ruler. That worthy person was Commander Kapilendra Dev, who, according to the *Madalapanji*, the temple chronicle of Puri *Srimandira*, could endear himself to Ganga king *Matta* Bhanudev such that he named him his successor. In the absence of Gangaraj, the danger of invasion from the external enemy was looming large on the horizon from many fronts simultaneously, and many vassal kings averse to him began stoking anarchy. Then some unseen power that always stood by the people saw that Bhanudev was unfit for Odisha's throne; a brave warrior like Kapilendra alone was suitable. Kapilendra got the crown at Kruttibash *Katak* (on the temple premises of *Ekamra Lingaraj*). That moment was the most promising in the history of the kingdom of Odisha. At that juncture, he was born in the military skies of Bharatavarsha, a comet whose glittering scintillating light was indeed the incarnation for suppressing the growing numbers of heretic Yavanas in the then society. Those Muslim forces were capturing Hindu kingdoms and were goaded by the one basic principle of destroying temples, forcing religious conversion and corrupting the native culture. They extended their empire in this way. Besides, they terrified the Bharatavarsha with their long-established practice of oppressing their subjects, violating women, and showing utter depravity towards sacred cows and the Brahmins. Even if a handful of Hindu kingdoms in Odisha, Vijayanagara and Rajaputana were conspicuous who could take action, they confined themselves to the defence of their domains only. They waited for self-defence as and when there was an attack on them. But Kapilendra Deva raised his sword and crushed these enemies ruthlessly.

Kapilendra Deva renovated and revived Odisha's army on the strength of kingdom resources. He used human resources and military components to re-organize the Odia army.

He spent three decades of his life on the battlefield. He kept a close watch on infiltrators from the Banga, Andhra and Telangana kingdoms who nibbled away the frontiers of the Kalinga-Utkal Kingdom that spread from Ganga to Godavari, from Kalinga Sea to Amarakantak. He was waiting for an opportunity to pounce upon them. Time and chance favour the brave. It fell in Kapilendra Deva's hand at the most opportune moment, and he applied it sagaciously.

After that, the Odisha Empire expanded itself, not simply from Ganga to Godavari but Krishnaveni and beyond; it was beyond Kaveri to Kanyakumari, the southernmost tip of Bharatavarsha figuring a vast territory of throbbing with aliveness. The elephantry of Odisha kept ramming everywhere in Bharatavarsha and continued marching throughout the Deccan.

The Odisha of 1464 A.D spread from the Ganges to *Setubandha*, the bridge of rocks Sri Rama of Ramayana built in the sea from Bharatavarsha to Sri Lanka. In the pages of history, the happy Odisha had extended its border to the farthest. And Gajapati Kapilendra Deva was its most successful architect, the most decisive leader of the people, the patron of a refined culture and a brilliant social and military organizer.

But what an irony! The history of Bharatavarsha has yet to give him his appropriate place. The country's history has taken a few incidents related to him and has mentioned him in a bit of space, so it has ignored the Gajapati dynasty, which ruled for at least a hundred years. Gajapati Kapilendra Deva marched with his elephantry in the country and defeated all those foreign rulers demolishing the Hindu civilization. His famous son, Purushottama Deva, was invincible for three decades, and his elite grandson Prataparudradev was a paragon of virtues who held the reins of the kingdom for four decades. The scripts on the Cuttack Gopinathpur temple, the copper plates of Raghudevpur close to Rajamahendry, the rock inscriptions at Warangal, and innumerable writings on the bodies of temples are pretty intelligible. History of India has conveniently ignored the Gajapati dynasty and its imperial saga.

The novel "Gajapati Kapilendra Deva and His Mastodon Power" presents a vivid portrayal of Gajapati Kapilendra Deva and his life, delving into both his remarkable accomplishments and the trials he faced towards the end of his reign. It provides the readers with a glimpse into the historical context and the challenges and triumphs of this influential ruler. This work is a narrative that combines history and fiction to bring to life the legacy of Gajapati Kapilendra Deva, shedding light on the man behind the powerful ruler.

The author expresses his heartfelt gratitude and deep appreciation for the invaluable assistance in translating his Odia book "Digvijoyi Gajapati" into English to Prof. M. S. Rao and Sri Rajendra Kumar Samal, renowned figures in English and Odia literature. Dr. Rao, your scholarly insights and deep understanding have been instrumental in ensuring accuracy and clarity of the translation. Mr. Samal, your poetic sensibility has added unique dimension to this book.

Indramani Jena
Samaroh, 128, Dumduma (A), Khandagiri,
Bhubaneswar, Odisha, India. 751030
Mobile – 9438007509

CONTENTS

Characters in this Book

Gajapati – Kapilendra Deva; Empress – Rupambika; Paramour Queen – Parvati,
Crown Prince – Hamvir Deva; Ordinary Prince – Purusottama Deva

Mahapatras or Ministers:

Mukhya or Chief Minister	-	Kasinath Mahapatra
Defence Minister	-	Gopinath Mahapatra
Antaranga Mahapatra	-	Uchhabaa Bairiganjana (Home Minister)
Sandhivigraha Mahapatra	-	Tribrikrama Samaresh (War and External Affair Minister) Mukuta Bahubalendra (War and External Affair Minister)
Antaranga Mahapatra	-	Sudarsana Rathsharma (Cultural Minister)
Pratirakshya Mahaparta	-	Bhima Bhujabala (Defence Minister)
Prashasanika Mahapatra	-	Digvijaya Pattanayak (Administration Minister)
Rajaguru Mahapatra	-	Shankara Acharya (Royal Advisor)
Raja Purohita	-	Laxmana Mahapatra (Royal Priest)

Parichhas (Governors) or Administrators:

Parichha of Gauda Kingdon	-	Jaleswara Narendra Mahapatra;
Parichha of Rajamahendry	-	Raghudeva Narendra Mahapatra;
Parichha of Kondavidu	-	Ganadev Routray;
Parichha of Chandragiri and Vijayanagara	-	Dakshineswara Kumara Mahapatra;
Parichha of Udayagiri	-	Tuma Bhupala;

Other Odisha Office Bearers:

Manager of Simadri Fort	-	Sudarsana Dakshinakabata;
Port Manager of Kalingapatana	-	Birupakshya Gajendra;
Manager of Koleru Gajapati Fort	-	Ratnakara Gumansingh
Minor Characters –		
Amat Narayana Mahapatra	-	Minister (Brother of Gopinath Mahapatra)
Dharani Uttarakabata	-	*Dagara* or Messenger

The Victorious Emperor

On a Sunday morning in summer of 1464 AD, marking the thirtieth year of Gajapati Kapilendra Deva's rule, the victorious Emperor returned to his Fort palace at Barabati in Cuttack. He had been away on many long and challenging expeditions in South India, tirelessly leading his military campaigns.

With the Emperor's return, the royal family was bustling with activity, eagerly awaiting their guardian's homecoming. The palace maintenance was working diligently to refurbish the nine-courted palace of Barabati, preparing to welcome the triumphant Commander who had been away on extensive campaigns in the southern regions. Although the turmoil in the south had subsided, Yubaraj Hamvira remained vigilant, overseeing the newly acquired territories.

Emperor Kapilendra Deva was not a man to be taken lightly. His demeanour was marked by a stubborn expression and a commanding booming voice. While he had a rare capacity for sweetness in his words, his voice could convey the harshest truths, instilling fear in those who heard it. His prominent mustache added to his military appearance, and he was known for his serious and unyielding temperament.

But he is very light today and called his room attendant sweetly, "Biku, come here. Are you listening to the murmuring crowd from a distance?"

"Yes, my lord," replied Biku, the old man with a dhoti and pyjama was Gajapati royal employee.

"Have you seen who they are?" asked the Gajapati Emperor of Odisha, the vibrating kingdom of the eastern coasts of India.

"Let me verify, Your Highness", replied Bikalananda and took leave.

The Commander stood up from his cane chair to examine the pictures of some local animals hanging on the wall. He noticed a *patachitra* in the east wall of his room, a robust black tusker in a military outfit. It faced south and enthusiastically lifted its left front leg about two cubits. It is the pose of a tusker when it attempts to squeeze anything.

"Who has posted this picture in my room?" asked the Commander to himself. He could not remember it was already there for a long. It was new to him now how he could not grasp its significance earlier, even if it were there! It is meaningful and indicates the glory of Odishan tusker in south expeditions.

"Who is the artist of Raghurajpur who designed and presented this grand art to the palace? It is not mere *patachitra* but a certain forecast!" exclaimed the Commander.

In the meantime, Biku had come back with some information. He told the Commander, "Your Majesty, the great winner, your subjects have stood before the nine-courtyard Navatala Palace to greet you with a cartload of bouquets, ornaments, dresses and gifts."

"Ask them to get into the assembly hall," the Commander paused.

"I must meet them at once. Go and, with the help of *Antaranga* Mahapatra, arrange the assembly hall. I shall be reaching there soon," said the Commander, and the royal dresser took no time to dress the king in Odishi silk residential attire and placed the Royal Crown on the head of His Highness.

"No, no! No crown in the group; I am going to be jubilant. I am not going to the Gajapati court to deliver a verdict or meet a visiting king or ambassador. I will meet the local subjects who love me as their dearest. The crown overhead will be a barrier to our natural affection for each other!" explained the Commander.

He saw all known faces on his way to the assembly hall. All his Mahapatras (Ministers) and political Patras (Advisors) were in the front row. Many royal employees were managing the crowd. The crowd was composed mainly of political elites of Odisha from subsidiary *Samanta* states. They had arrived here to greet their Gajapati, the victorious Emperor.

Heaps of bouquets adorned his decorated table with many costly yellow metal gifts. The assembly hall had the fragrance of sandalwood in the air.

The arrival of the Emperor hushed up the audience in the hall. With the initial slogan from the front row, the rhythm of "Hurrah! Our victorious commander" echoed repeatedly.

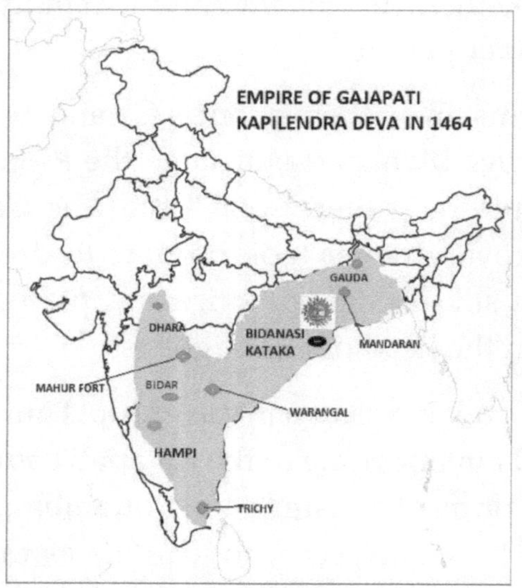

Map of this year, 1464 speaks of Gajapati's Achievements

With a joyful face, which looked full and fulfilling, the Emperor waved his hands to greet the enthusiastic crowd. Paused for a while for the silence to return and spoke, "It is the grace of the Trinity to make all these happen. Where is the tiny General of the Ganga Army, and where is the vast Odisha Rashtra to take shape? Can it be possible by human efforts? It is all providence that has played. Without Lord Jagannath's grace, human efforts would never have made the convincing victory possible. And this vast territory of Odisha today could never take shape with me as a tiny General. You, all my benevolent subjects and great participants in the efforts of the Gajapati Army, need to be greeted before anybody else. United, we have been successful in warding off the undesirable invaders and expanding our territory just as well."

There was grand applause from the crowd with claps and 'God is Great' utterances. The entire audience bowed in salutation with folded hands.

The Emperor continued, "At every step of our journey, some miracle happened, so much so that our enemy could overestimate our military capability. We were a terror to the enemy and a nightmare for the rulers of the southern kings and vassals. Do you imagine who was the source of my strength?

"No, you can't imagine. It was some hidden force that was playing all along with me. His presence made me stronger than I was. I had no instance of looking back or front. Only my target and available force were at my forefront. I could not foresee what was going to happen next. It is my destiny that led my way to victory.

"The mystical force that always encouraged me to proceed boldly was Lord Jagannath, who was leading me all along."

With an exaggerated feeling of joy, he emphasized that the land he was born is adventurous. It has the heritage of mastering the marine trade and colonizing the *Subarna Dwipa*, the island countries in the Far East. A new name Odisha was emerging out of Kalinga. Kalinga had mightiness with its natural forces, the force of its black elephants. It was one Alexander who could humble and train one wild unruly horse, and with that, he became the world conqueror. So the Kings and Emperors of Kalinga perceived that with the trained elephants, they could conquer the whole of Bharatavarsa.

He shouted, "Time favoured me to serve my motherland with the weapons she had. Favourable circumstances made me sail smoothly in the turbulent ocean of this running century, and I ascribe it as a blessing of the grandest Lord looking at us with his staring eyes."

Gajapati, the actual Commander of the elephant forces of Odisha, stood silent, filled with sublime emotions and exhilarated with phenomenal success and with drops of joyful tears trickling down his eyes. He saluted with folded hands facing the south, the direction of Lord Jagannath, the Grand deity of the state.

The entire assembly was quiet. Everyone was stunned by the humility of the great warrior king, who did not boast about his achievements but gave credit the Lord Jagannath, who was responsible for all his victories. The Commander looked like a strong warrior with a stout appearance, military moustache and facies but was an infant before the Lord of the land.

A murmur that gradually grew louder, 'Jay Jagannath', 'Jay Jagannath', the usual respectful appreciation of the sons of the soil echoed the hall.

Gajapati Kapilendra

The meeting ended, and the crowd dispersed. But the *Antaranga* Mahapatra, the Minister of royal affairs, rushed down to the dispersing assembly, contacted a few other Ministers and intimated to them that there would be a royal meeting next week. Kindly take note of it. As the functioning of the benevolent

Gajapati had been on a war expedition for a long time, he wanted to get the feedback of his kingdom through your statements.

Now Gajapati had time to relax for some days as the aches of long horse rides were healing slowly. But the pleasant memories of his movement and triumphs one after another were crowding his thought. Now he had no desire to go for any further expedition. He had attained a military equilibrium with all neighbouring forces, and it would be obsessive if he aspired to invade distant kingdoms.

He had a great curiosity in the core of his heart. How could he have such a capability at an advanced age? He did not believe his achievements as pure luck and God's gift. He was a firm believer in work psychology. A purposeless mind does not deserve any progress. Something inherent in him guided his strategic movements.

Many events of past years rolled down in his memory. It was a day when he got to estimate the military strength of Ganga king *Matta* Bhanudev. The state's military Commander was disorganized as an inattentive and leisure-seeking last Ganga King. A substantial military force of mighty Ganga Kings centuries back was shrinking and had tailed down to a meagre size.

The elephantry wing of Ganga Forces was deteriorating. He was recruited and realized it. The negligent Ganga grandsons rapidly diminished the grand tradition of Anangabhimadev or Narasimha Deva.

Not far off, he could come to know details from his father, Jageswar Nayak, who was a reputed custodian of the Elephant Squad of Gangas. He had preliminary knowledge of Elephantry as his home trade. The elephant mahout in Odisha elephantry was called Sahani, and the cavalry rider as Rout. His father was in overall charge of the war elephants. That was how he got huge inspiration from his father.

Before his recruitment in the elephantry division of his father, he listened to his father's teachings. His father welcomed him on the day he joined the Ganga military squad. Jageswar felt contented with his son for his recruitment. His family's third generation of military services aroused immense pride in his mind.

"*Abhinandan*, my son, congratulations! You have been selected by your perseverance, not by family reputation," said his father, the custodian of Odisha elephantry.

"You must be aware", his father continued, "present military status of the Ganga kingdom has deteriorated to a great extent. Gangapati today is blind to his boundary, so also to his forces. There needs to be a solution in the maintenance of the fighting machine. But within the three active wings of our troops, we chiefs have sworn in to continue recruitment and training in apprehension of neighbours' attacks.

"The feudal pattern of warriors, with their main job as agriculture, removes the performance in war fields. Long intervals of peace degenerate the skill of the traditional war force of a kingdom. From the days of Narasimha Deva, about two centuries ago, Odisha had not faced any attack nor organized one to infiltrate the north or south neighbour. Rather, its fragmented and resting army has merged with the normal population, and this weakness has encouraged the south so much that the Reddys and the Vijayanagara had eaten away one-third of Odisha."

Now the succeeding Commander recollects how he reacted to his father's bitter comment. He had asked him a question that aroused him from his interior, "Father, is there a way to tide over this problem?"

"O sure, my son, this kingdom is a battlefield, where none other than warriors inhabit. Here the mahouts trap the wild elephants and train them as the most aggressive tuskers of the frontline division. About one thousand eight hundred years back, even Vishnugupta cautioned the mighty Emperor Chandragupta Maurya to take note of the powerful black tuskers of Kalinga. Kalingans would be hard to conquer."

Young Kapilendra was delighted when he learnt that the elephant of his native land is mighty, so much so that no other elephant would be more invincible on the battlefield than Odisha's. During the last thousand and eight hundred years, he was curious to know the king who had tamed the war and earned high honour for the motherland. He was too interested and could not resist the temptation to know.

"Father, was there any crowned head of this soil who had organized his elephants to empower the kingdom?" asked a weary voice from within the intuitive young military recruitee Kapilendra.

"Sure", answered Father, "there are a handful of potentates who believed in elephant power. But very few were themselves experts to tackle one elephant and could command war on a war elephant."

The young mind could not believe against his conception that Commander-in-chief, not the king, was commanding the war. He now grasped that a king could lead his troop. He was satisfied. He was curious to know the monarchs who were masters of the great military potential of the soil.

Father could guess why his son is quiet. He intentionally delayed to break the silence.

"Can I know about them?" came a query in a low voice from an excited mind.

Father was amazed by the intuitiveness of his son, who had just joined the defence forces of Ganga elephants. He felt the family and the nation welcomed his ambitions. He wished to put forth exhaustive shreds of evidence on Odishan elephants and the momentum the Elephantry had reached in the past.

Father Jageswar advised him to visit two places, with one month gap, *Ekamra Kanan* and *Arka-Kshetra*, to have first-hand experience on elephant warfare. But in the meantime, this ambitious newcomer received some preliminary training. The most accomplished *Sahani* (mahout) of the elephantry taming and teaching wing was called upon to teach the new youth about war elephants.

Aranya Sahani was the veteran elephant mahout in charge of the youth Kapil for arousing interest in elephant power. He felt that the Elephantry dominated the war alongside the infantry, artillery and cavalry. It was Elephantry, the heavy-weight war tank that foreruns the main force as *Aguani Thata* or forward troops in Odisha's military forces. Sahani imparted the art of catching a wild tusker from dense forests that stretched from Ekamra Kanan to Chudanga Gada, interiors of Odisha's hilly tracts, the *Garjats*, Jharakhanda and Bastar area in the West. Wild tuskers were trapped and trained. Only the robust and aggressive male elephants, the tuskers, were imparted special training by an expert from the Ganga military trainers in the interiors of dense jungles where feeding the elephants was easy. The tuskers received satisfactory training, then recruited to the Elephant Commands of Ganga Elephantry stationed at Odishan borders or the Castles and Forts maintained by the royal administration.

Young Kapilendra had a few doubts before his

apprenticeship in Elephantry. After training, all his doubts were gone.

"How many war elephants are ordinarily maintained by Ganga kings? Give me the figure of my ideal, Narasimha Deva, two hundred years ago", asked the apprentice politely.

"Ordinarily, one and a half to two thousand war tuskers were part of an expeditious Ganga military forces of Narasimha Deva. The figure often declined with idle descendant Ganga kings who had no interest in military action", replied the trainer.

"What was the use of many she elephants in the Ganga military?" asked an anxious apprentice.

"No female elephant is recruited to the forward troop of Elephantry that pierces the enemy's barrier. Cow elephants have no place in battle-ready positions. The cows are no doubt faithful in transporting war materials," was the reply of the mahout Aranya.

"Bull elephants of different ages might not have been useful for war. Which is the optimal age of a war tusker?" asked the young enthusiastic apprentice.

The experienced mahout was startled. Such an unexpected and pertinent nosey question had never been asked by anyone earlier. The new apprentice has a brilliant chance to lead the elephantry. Such a question asks to satisfy the deep thirst to maintain the elephantry's efficiency level. In a setting of thousand and five hundred war tuskers, most fit for war at fifty-five to sixty-five years of age, a chain of one hundred and fifty tuskers must be ready to enter every year, with a similar number retiring from the military. The mahout gave his concept to the apprentice to satisfy his curiosity and quench his thirst for learning.

He also gave a short narrative that the last Ganga King, *Matta* Bhanudev, had a rare interest in the military and had never war with any infiltrator of the Odishan boundary. He had little foresight, and even the maintenance of the elephant force was the job of the elephantry stock house; Jageswar Nayak, the apprentice's father, was keen enough to maintain the chain of introducing new elephants to the Ganga army every year. The Ganga military lost its roots and identity during the last few generations. Shouts of infiltration and war march-past were audible to Odisha, not only from north Illyas Sahis of Bengal but also from the independent Muslim ruler of Jaunabad, Malwa in the West and the Rajamahendry Reddys from the south.

A young apprentice could not digest this statement; he was restless about converting this ill-omen into an active medium of solidarity in his motherland.

"Is anything being done to maintain our mastodon forces?" he asked worriedly.

"Don't worry, my dear; we rightly maintain our bull forces with the meagre revenue grants! We are sure our motherland will face a grave disaster instantaneously without this. Your father is the pacemaker of elephant force equilibrium. He gets worried if there is any scarcity in the annual recruitment of young boars to the elephantry", replied Sahani.

"Oh!" murmured the young apprentice as a mark of satisfaction.

Jogeswar Nayak, the Commandant of Ganga elephantry, felt satisfied that his third son, Kapilendra, had grasped the pace of military power of his motherland, and he decided to spend some time demonstrating the miracles of mammoth power. He thought that his son was quite enthusiastic and determined in temperament. Kapilendra did not involve himself in any worthless affair. Once he could get glimpses of the achievements of the tuskers of his motherland, he would be a great commander of the elephant forces one day.

Jageswar told his son to accompany him on an elephant ride. One fine morning they started early from their military camp at Chudanga Gada towards Ekamra Kanan on the western outskirts of Bhubaneswar. It was only a few kroshas (one krosh is two miles or 3 kilometres) away. They had with them Mahavir Upadhyaya, a military guide of their squad.

They climbed the minor hill on the northern side. People name it by its traditional name, Kumarigiri, the hill of princesses recently called Udayagiri or the hill of sunrise. Only after a short distance, Kapilendra was new to notice habitable caves. He was astonished at the rows of shelters with architectural beauty on the walls.

"The caves here were once the abode of Jain Arhats of Kalinga, and this Kumarigiri is the brainchild of a mighty emperor who ruled the Greatest Kalinga", started chauffeur Mahavir. "The Emperor's exact name is unknown, but people of the locality call him *Ayur Maharaj*. He had carved all his achievements in the stone walls of the caves more than one millennium ago. But it is meaningful to its spectator. The eastern road in front of the residential caves of Jain monks leads to a palace. Follow me to behold the glorious past of this kingdom."

They reached the palace named by locality as *Ranigumpha* or the Queen's Cave. All of them were breathtakingly bewildered at the artistic vitality of the cave in such a dense forest! Young Kapilendra moved to touch the petroglyphs. He needed more time to interpret the cave arts and motifs.

He took a thorough round on the ground floor. The guide explained all the depictions in the walls and columns. Kapilendra, for whom his father arranged the trip, was quite thirsty for knowledge of the artistic interpretations of the chauffeur.

The mansion of caves was unique in the world at the time of its making when no temple existed. The Ayur King had employed thousands of Kalinga stone-workers and cave artists to dig the burrows in the body stone of the hill, carve symbolic art pictures and even inscribe brief indications in contemporary scripts.

"So great and enthusiastic our forefathers millennia ago!" exclaimed the young military recruitee. "Uncle Upadhaya, please go on elaborately with all your knowledge and experience. You must have come here so many times. You might know what local people and Bhubaneswar pundits know about this place. Please proceed slowly to be grasped easily by me."

"You see, this emperor has done miracles with the mammoth power of his motherland", replied Upadhyaya.

He continued, "The architecture in ground floor caves of *Ranigumpha* indicates elephant march towards the north and a spirited display of Kalinga power by the then Kalinga Emperor, the Ayur King. Such a vast Kalinga military troop headed by strong black Kalinga tuskers had widened its boundaries in all possible directions.

Again, the mighty Magadha king of the north, was compelled to surrender to *Kalingadhipati* Ayur King, and the victorious Emperor returned with Kalinga Jina, the state deity of Kalinga; you note this picture on the northern wall of the Queen's Cave. This is the pictorial representation of how the Magadha King, Brihaspati Mitra, saluted Ayur Kharavela bending down on his knees."

The guide tried to convince his tourists with all experience he had gathered. He convinced them this climate was rich in breeding quality elephants that Chandragupta Maurya, the greatest Maurya, was morally afraid of. Kalingans had extraordinary elephant power and could do anything to overwhelm an enemy.

Kapilendra, by now, was convinced of the powerfulness of *Kalingadhipati Ayur* King. He skilfully applied the mastodon power to the Odia troops. But he had a dozen more questions about *Kalingadhipati*, who ruled this land more than one millennium ago.

He continued, "What was the age of *Kalingadhipati* when he dreamt of inculcating stone-cut art and architecture here." Also, he pondered how strong the foot soldiers in his army were! He looked anxiously at the face of the chaperone.

Upadhyaya swung his head as if unsure about this issue and started, "Nobody knows the exact story, not even the locals here. But this cave art indicates Ayur Emperor had a robust army of four wings, infantry, cavalry, war chariots and elephantry. Rare few Kalingan rulers had an expeditious temperament. The temperament of the

Ayur king is quite remarkable in the Queen's cave stone arts. He had a vast military competent enough to bend down any prominent ruler of his time and return with triumph. He was a masterpiece of bravery and military posture."

It was convincing for the young tourist that his motherland could produce a military leader with war elephants moving freely in its dense forests. The leader who could manage these stout animals in the war field could overpower the enemy.

He was assertive. He could learn a tactic that was the key to his success in life as a General in the elephantry of Odisha.

They camped for two days at the hillside to explore the manifold achievements of the unknown Kalinga Emperor. Strange, he was an art lover, a great playwright, a patriot and a lover of all religions. Kapilendra had this favourite Emperor of the motherland seated on his crown in his mind. He overstayed half a day more to revisit some essential caves inside the arts of military excellence, elephant cravings and war scenes.

The last rock art he saw was on the upper story of the Queen's cave. An emperor riding a lion with a prominent main. Probationer Kapilendra's fascination reflects his awe and admiration for the emperor's depicted might and grandeur. It profoundly influenced him and he was fully amazed.

Lion-rider, Emperor Kharavela

To gain deeper understanding of the significance of the picture, Kapilendra calls upon Upadhyaya, their spot guide. Upadhyaya proceeds to explain he context of the image, revealing that the Ayur king's ministerial council along with his *Singhapatha* queen, Sindhula was in charge of supervising the exact recording of the cage art by the professionals. The Cave artisans got the achievements of the formidable *Mahameghavahana* emperor, who was known for his invincibility. His mere arrival would cause the foreign invaders leave this pious land. This historical context adds depth and meaning to the image, making it a symbol of the emperor's unmatched power and influence.

They left the twin hills, and the elephant carried them to *Ekamra Kshetra*. The new tourist found the place quite crowded, with Shaivites offering their worship at different temples. They visited Kruttibash Temple, Ananta-Basudeva Temple near Bindusagara Lake, Kedara-Gouri and Rajarani Temple. The Father of Kapilendra was convinced of the architectural dominance of Odisha, which the Somavamsi Kesari dynasty and Gangavamsi Kings had emphatically maintained.

Kapilendra was amazed by the number of temples of Ekamra and asked his father, who could think of building so many temples around this religious settlement?

Bewildering Temple City, Ekamra Bhubaneswar

Before his father could instruct anything, Upadhyaya, the guide, said to Kapilendra that so many kings had their presence here at Ekamra. No doubt, this was Toshali, a great town since immemorial, even when Ashok fought the battle of the Kalinga War here. Ashok has built so many Buddhist stupas and digging of Bindusagara Pond since then. Those structures did not stand, and the great storm had buried down much before the coronation ceremony of the Ayur King at Sisupalagada, the capital palace of old Kalinganagari. These buried and shaped stones could be identified as a stone from netherworlds, representing deities and kings who heard this were constructing sizeable temples over an unearthed stone. Ekamra was full of temples a few centuries ago, and that was how this temple town was named Bhubaneswar.

"You see, all these were the outcome of victorious Kalinga, you say, Odisha. The resources behind this lavish architecture were from the war-win booties of the Great Ganga King, Narasimha Deva. Our temple construction centuries coincide with our maritime excellence and the donation of our maritime merchants called the *Sadhavas*", explained Father Jageswar.

He was full of high-spirited delight and felt lifted to dreams, "Have I the wings of an Odisha King, I would startle the world with my dream of events".

Then their team travelled to Konark to get some impression of the elephant power of the land. They turned around the Sun Temple and were amazed by the technique and the design of its walls. Konark was only one hundred and fifty years old and growing with all its artistic emissions.

"My son, you appreciate the craftsmanship of Odisha. You note the metallic Sun God floats in this temple, and the first ray of Sun never fails to inundate Him! Mark the iron used in the temple and the accurate Sun Watch in its premises indicating Time. Every fingerbreadth of the temple wall of Konark not only radiates its uniqueness but reminds every spectator of its historical background." After this communication, his father took a few short breaths.

"I am amazed to see the proud lions crushing the elephant in the temple's front gate. What does it signify?" queried Kapilendra.

"So far as I know, though it is Sun Temple, built on Mahabharata epic evidence of Sun God making Samba, son of Lord Krishna, free from the cursed leprosy disorder, it has the great impression of its builder, Narasimha Deva's astute aggressive policy against the core enemy and his victory over them. Indeed Konark lion crushing the elephant is a superpower. Here Narssimhadev is the lion and Nawab of Champa, Bangala is not less powerful than an elephant," Father completed his remarks.

As an apprentice in Ganga forces, Kapilendra could not think further. He dreamt of being a part of the lion to chase upon the enemy of the motherland, how mighty he might be. His courage needs ways and means of expression. Then puzzles crowded his thoughts. He could not visualize a way to beat the armed Afghan soldiers of Bangala Nawab, the infiltrators of the southern boundary of the motherland.

But one doubt crept into the mind of the enthusiastic young probationer on what was the achievement of Gangaraj Narasimha Deva to celebrate his victory with such a permanent precious temple of the Sun God? He was momentarily hesitant whether he should ask his father about it.

"I am astonished by the temple built here. But what did our Gangaraj achieve to have this victory monument?" finally asked the probationer.

Then the royal chauffeur Upadhyaya was prompt without any delay in this query. He said, "This matter is the talk of our Ganga Sena. He was a dynamic Ganga king in his administrative process. Narasimha Deva was not tolerant of neighbours frequently infiltrating Odisha from the north border to loot the temple treasury of Lord Jagannath at Purusottama Kshetra. The Afghan Nawab who occupied Bangala at the time was a habitual plunderer of temples of our homeland. Gangaraj strengthened our northern gate at Mandaran, but despite it, the process of ransacking continued unabated. He consulted all the generals of his military engagement and invaded the infiltrator's domain. Ganga army took an invasive role and taught the Afghan ruler Tughril-Tughan Khan such a lesson even his monarch from Delhi could not save the kingdom from the clutches of Odia Paikas. This invasive role had a good diplomatic process of capturing one of their white Afghan elephants and making the Muslim army get lured into Odisha territory to be trapped.

His name is real Narasimha, a man-looking lion," Upadhyaya completed his explanation.

Kapilendra all on a sudden gazed at the lion gate of Konark Temple. The two lions on the sides of the gate were about the emblem overriding the elephant. The youngman was filled with the curiosity about it significance. Accompanying guide, Upadhyaya explained the might and war tactics employed by Gangaraj Narasimha Deva over Afghan Bengal ruler represented his prowess and capability.

Konark Temple Lion Gate Image

He continued to gaze upon the emblem, began to grasp the idea that one's capability and ambition can lead to a great achievement. This realisation kindles a sense of optimism and determination within him, symbolised by the rising sun in his mental horizon. It signifies the dawn of his aspirations and the belief that he can achieve as much as he desires and works towards

The probationer, Kapilendra, felt fulfilled and satisfied. This short trip to Kumarigiri, Ekamra, and Konark had augmented his vision beyond elephantry and power. He dreamt of being the Chief of Gangasena and creating miracles for Odisha. Now he had two ideals before him, the omnipotent Ayur King of Kumarigiri and the tactful expeditious Narasimha Deva, the architect of Konark. He was reluctant to speak out but preferred to be a robust expeditious Chief of Gangasena. The seed of such an army started germinating in his mind from this day.

Many years have passed with promotion to the prestigious General of Ganga Elephantry position. His managerial capacity was evident, so much so that it came to the knowledge of Gangaraj *Matta* Bhanudev.

It was not far off. Gangaraj invited him to Barabati Palace to entrust him with the task of dealing with infiltrating neighbours. Strangely due to luck or chance, the General could effectively negotiate in north and south borders. The relationship with the General was so conspicuous that anyone at that time considered him the closest link to Gangaraj, and even some expected him to be the next Ganga King.

With this much progress in his thought, he was disturbed by the sweet memories of his Mahapatras, who assembled at his Conference Hall to greet him - his day passed by with the ceremony of garlanding him with felicitation from all corners of Odisha.

As such, he is not a man to be exhilarated by the sweet flattering voice of any Minister or tall talker. Nobody grasped the miraculous achievement. Nobody knew the invisible strength of the Gajapati Army. It was the citadel of motivated military power.

The felicitation ceremony lasted for half a day. As a person close to the Gajapati, only Gopinath Mahapatra stayed behind to spend the evening in the fat Castle of Barabati.

It was the 30th *Kapilabda* (the year 1464); the day of the year was the same as the lunar calendar of Lord Jagannath when Gopinath had a leading role in declaring Kapilendra as a new Sovereign.

There was minimal discussion between them, but the room had an environment of satiety. Mahapatra felt elated as he was behind the success of what Odisha had witnessed for many years. Things had taken shape over time; these thirty years had drawn all possible gains for the motherland. It was nothing but luck on the side of the first Gajapati of Odisha, whose every touch turned basal metal into gold.

Kapilendra noticed a smile of satisfaction radiating from the grave face of Mahapatra.

"What was in your mind, my friend Gopinath?" asked the Gajapati in a low voice.

"I note how fast the time has passed!" replied Mahapatra Gopinath.

"It is not faster than the speed of war-tuskers of our motherland," emphasized Gajapati.

"Sure, if you are quoting the speed of our tusker attacking Bahamani General at Devarakonda," added Gopinath, "Even a waterfall from a mountain can't gain that speed. Our robust bulls could reach there within minutes before the enemy could think of attacking, and they paid the price as our enemy."

"I will say boldly, you have a strong hand in this success," slowly replied the Gajapati.

"No, my honourable Gajapati, I was all along here; how can I make my face south when you entrust me the northern border," replied Gopinath.

"That's right. But who advised me of the sermon of gathering mammoth strength of Odisha? Tell me, who is my competent Mahapatra to find strategic locations bordering Odisha throughout the country? Also, tell me, who is he who is in charge of preparing our winning flags of amber colour?" Gajapati completed his statement and looked cheerfully at Gopinath.

"It's time that responded, not full credit of any of your Mahapatras. General Kapilendra had proved his competence. And he was crowned King of Odisha, Premier Gajapati of his dynasty. Following that day, Odisha has been reaping the best harvests daily for the last 30 years. The development is all around the kingdom. People murmur among themselves that a golden era has ushered in Gajapati's spontaneous actions and broad vision from the 'Odisha Rashtra' of his dream," replied Gopinath.

"It is all due to your focus on one point. You have stressed Elephantry as a great weapon since our confidential meeting. Though I am a proponent of this concept and had formal training, I got a strong impetus from your support. We have worked out our need and execution border-wise and the smooth management of our mastodon military asset. You have also worked for our southern limits and neighbours in addition to the northern limits," concluded Gajapati in one breath.

"Thank you, my Lord; I am amazed; you have emerged from Suryavansha, the Sun dynasty, and your additional title of 'Gajapati' acknowledges your mastery of the accumulated tusker strength of our kingdom. Channelizing power of wild elephants in the field of war is as old as Mahabharata and beyond. But your acceptance and revival have resulted in the country's infallible massive power reserve. Only some Hindu Kings of India can face foreign infiltrators from the western border of India. The strong Hindu rulers of India could overcome the tyrant killers from the West, but they engulfed small kingdoms. We are proud of you and your role model, erstwhile Narasimha Deva, who built the Konark Temple and had a strong will to disarray the spreading of foreign power. You have the ability and courage to attack the foreign infiltrators, mostly in South India, whereas Narasimha Deva had his eyes set on the north and south. I pray with folded hands to Lord Jagannath to give still more strength to your Majesty to maintain this Gajapati Empire founded by you," concluded Gopinath in a prayerful gesture.

But Gajapati was looking at the image of the Lord on the *Patachitra* cloth hung on the right wall of his room. He was a bit emotional, and tears of joy came from his eyes.

"You see, Lord, expressed through you to maintain power in the kingdom's interior and newly acquired territory. You are a senior Senapati of the Ganga King, and your progeny have been involved in the military services for so many generations of Ganga rule. You have used all your intellect to save your homeland from enemies. You have also efficiently managed the Gajapati Army that took over the Gangasena. Gangasena was in top order during Narasimha Deva but degenerated into a miserable state by our time. You have revitalized it by your foresight," Kapilendra Deva said satisfactorily.

"Who am I? It is the grace of the Lord. You appeared in between to occupy the throne and to save the state deity and the state from imminent danger. I am always with you. I know you have enough experience with elephant power. I applied my know-how to make an army reserve at all weak spots of our elongated Odisha that is highest by this year, 20th *Kapilabda* (1464 AD). You maintain all components, the elephants, cavalry and foot soldiers at all our strategic Forts, Borders.

"I commend your idea of maintaining a mobile prompt ever-ready army around Krishna River. It has yielded good results. You could reach within no time to throttle the enemy. Prompt response is a virtue of great strategic importance that history will remember forever."

Gajapati, with a sense of satisfaction in his expression, stated, "It is all grace of Lord Jagannath, who is the Ganga General Kapilendra, and where is Gajapati's throne? All these are incredible. When I could see these with my eyes, I decided to make myself like Narasimha Deva, who thought of him as Gajapati but couldn't affix this title to his name. I have added this title to the Kings of Odisha, who stand over the credit of elephants even at this juncture.

"The infiltrators are afraid of our trained elephants. Even if we have two thousand war tuskers, the Bahamani rulers figure it as two lakhs and retreat from the battlefield on our very appearance. That is a perfect strategy for winning battles," uttered Gajapati with a boastful smile.

Both rejoiced with some royal cuisine. Gajapati was looking very closely at his comrade Gopinath Mahapatra, a dedicated General of the northern border who belonged to the family loyal to Odisha and Gangarajas for the last three centuries.

"Gopinath, you are so gifted and foresighted and dependable in our midst. I am lucky in getting you in our midst. I don't bother about the repeated attacks of Bangla Nawab and the Ruler of Jaunabad; the Gangaraj *Matta* Bhanudev disappeared, creating a sense of terror among residents here. You have rightly involved the responsible heads of the kingdom to crown me at this juncture and ward off the northern intrusions. Despite the violent warmongers gritting their teeth, this competent General could ward off them. He has a substantial role in the victory of Gajapati over Gauda, Jaunabad and Delhi," an extended spectrum of thought kept running in the mind screens of the Gajapati.

The southern wing of the Gajapati army had the main ground of alertness in the centre of Deccan. That also involved the tremendous diplomatic and marshal wisdom of this giant. Every attack or defence undertaken by Gajapati Kapilendra had a well-advised concept of the special team headed by Gopinath Mahapatra.

Nobody could believe his luminous advice to dominate in South India; it had provided enough power to conquer all kingdoms of the south, including that of the rival Hindu Kingdom, Vijayanagara.

Once, you had whispered to me, "Your Majesty, listen to me. Have half of Odisha's military force deployed at Godavari or Krishna bank, and the chance will come to capture the whole of south India.

"I made no delay in accepting this attractive proposal. Since such a posting, we are reaping the successes and serving people as Gajapati power. We have bagged many kingdoms with administrative capitals during the last decade."

The Minister stood silently and observed the speech of Gajapati. Ardent Mahapatra did not feel delighted with the praise of Gajapati, a characteristic attribute of every traditional royal employee, as if it was only his duty.

A few Moments had passed, Gopinath bade farewell to Gajapati and sought his permission to leave the Fort.

Gajapati was elated in mind by congratulatory messages from all over India. He was a hero of the time, and everybody was boasting of his bravery.

In the meantime, Biku, the royal attendant, was waiting to convey some message.

"Your Highness, *Mukhya Mahapatra* (Chief Minister) Kasinath Mahapatra is waiting to meet you."

Arrange the meeting in the royal drawing room. I am reaching there within a few moments.

On arrival of Gajapati, Kasinath greeted him with a bunch of palm leaf documents and said, "Your Majesty's humble and obedient servant, Kasinath presents a treatise in complete colloquial Odia language written by Sarala Das. He is waiting outside for your orders to meet you. There are also some other Sanskrit writers."

"Biku, go and get the noble, learned writer to this front seat," asked the Gajapati.

Sarala Das, a simple person with traditional rural dress, was present before Gajapati. He saluted the Gajapati with folded hands and in the local style.

"You have done a wonder, my dear author of Odia Mahabharata. How could the Lord give you so much courage to perform this stupendous task? I am delighted with your great job for the Odia race. We were learning everything from Sanskrit texts and analyzing in our mind in Odia language; you have described Odisha's mountains, rivers and forests in the text of your Odia Mahabharata. You have done the right job, which neither other Odia nor learned Pundit had ever done. The Pundits and learned persons have emphasized Sanskrit, and no doubt that it enriches Sanskrit Literature and Culture. But many Odia-speaking races need this knowledge as Sanskrit texts are obscure. Poorly articulated Sanskrit Texts and Purans are not useful for ordinary Odia people," Gajapati put forth this appreciation.

"Please tell me your residential address, Author," asked the Gajapati.

I am Siddheswar Parida from Sarala Kshetra. I could accomplish this work only with the grace of Goddess Sarala. I have served in the Gajapati Army in the south. When I heard people in Telugu and other languages think of translating different epics like Ramayana and Mahabharata into their language. I decided to leave my job and prepare this text in a new style suitable for my people who did not know Sanskrit. The ideology of the great epic will enlighten you. Ramayana and Mahabharata have reformed the lifestyle of our people. To make it more popular in the broader circle, I have this endeavour for Odia race, and I pray your honour to inaugurate it."

"My congratulations to you, Great poet, Sarala Das! You are unique among Odias. You have a broad vision of a distant horizon. I can't see the long future, but one day it will stand as a great milestone in Odia literature, indicating an iceberg behind it. I know you are too broad in your mind and are a great spokesman for the Odia language. I declare Odia is our language here and accept Odia as today's official administrative language."

By order of Gajapati, Sarala Das was honoured with dignity, and Gajapati presented a royal memento to him for his stupendous work.

Sanskrit language teaching and research were part of Odishan education and culture. Sanskrit writers and dramas flourished in Odisha. These reached heights during the tenure of Gajapati Kapilendra Deva. Many Sanskrit writers were waiting to meet the honourable Gajapati.

Kasinath Mahapatra introduced Visvanath Kabiraj, who wrote the Sanskrit text *Sahitya Darpana* and Chandrakala Natika. The Gajapati appreciated these texts as a pride of Odisha. Narasingha Mishra Vajapeyi authored *Samksepasaririka Vartika* was appreciated by the Gajapati as it pertained to health aspects. Gajapati also honoured many other authors, including Narayan Chayani, who wrote *Sudhichandika*. Many authors received royal gifts and appreciative mementoes.

Many subjects from far and wide had assembled to meet Gajapati. Chief Minister Kasinath Mahapatra passed on the information to the Gajapati that a few aspirants are waiting for the grace of Gajapati. Gajapati called upon them to the conference hall. A number of them from Kapileswar near Bhubaneswar stood up and expressed with joy the completion of Lord Shiva's temple in their locality. They were lucky enough to have the blessings of the Gajapati, and he had enough affection and love for the poor. The locality was named Kapileswar after the Gajapati.

"I am proud of you, Kapileswar and Kapileswar Shaivite temple. He is an active God, and people have dreamt of the deity for a long time. The appearance of the Shiva Linga from underground moved me to complete the temple and develop the locality. This temple is a memorial of the architecture of the Gajapati era," was the appreciation of first Suryavamsi Gajapati.

A group of residents from Ekamra Bhubaneswar who profoundly liked Gajapati came to congratulate their leader. They were elderly adults and natives

Kapileswar Mahadev Temple

of Bhubaneswar. Some of them are servitors of Papanashini Temple, the exact site of the coronation of Gajapati Kapilendra in 1435. That was inscribed in Kruttibash Temple a few years later. There is an image in the Kapali Mutt. An inscription with Odia letters "Kapileswar Dev Raj" is there- this inscription appeared in 1452, during his 17 years of reign. The chief of the group, Kusun Badu, was neatly dressed and had a strong voice.

"We are very much delighted by witnessing how far you have reached. It is our good luck to be associated with your company even years before your coronation. God bless you, and you are our ideal king. We felt during the last three decades we are with you, as closely as we were at the time of your coronation", exclaimed Badu.

Gajapati has every bit of memory of what happened on his coronation day and the role of these local people as a tool of Minister Gopinath Mahapatra. He was happy and shared his happiness with them.

Here in that cultural gathering, there was an announcement by Chief Minister, Kasinath that on the occasion of *Chandan Yatra* in Purushottama (Puri), the drama Parshurama Vijaya written by His Highness Sri Sri Gajapati Kapilendra Deva will be staged inside the premises of *Srimandira*. There was a sense of appreciation for the learned gathering and colossal enthusiasm to be an eyewitness of the drama. There was a wave of praise for such an endeavour by the Gajapati, who was as powerful as Parshurama. The eagerness of the gathering compelled the Gajapati to speak a few words on his treatise.

"I feel proud of being born as an Odia. I have a strong mother tongue that its people have spoken since immemorial. The text form is of recent origin. But this soil has been a breeding ground of heroes and heroism. Look at the Ayur King of Udayagiri-Kumarigiri hills of Ekamra or the Gangaraj Narasimha Deva of Konark – they are my role models. I follow in their footsteps in every move I plan. So also is Parshurama in our Mahabharata. His heroism has no bounds. Parshurama is an inspiration for our race. Start and Progress, March and Achieve," with these short words, he concluded his speech.

Many servitors of *Srimandira* who were in

the audience of Gajapati Conference Hall were overwhelmed when they saw the dramatic presentation of Gajapati's 'Parshurama Vijaya' text. They wished for their participation and the successful staging of the Parshurama Vijaya. The hero of the epic is quite known to everyone. It will reinforce heroism in the minds of the spectators.

The conference did not end there. People from Kaunrpur and Gopinathpur of Cuttack expressed gratitude for the Dadhivamana temples constructed in their villages. He said his satisfaction and added a note, "I have little time in my life to think of any temple or architectural progress. My expedition had been non-stop for 30 years, from *Kapilabda* 1 (1434 AD) to 30th *Kapilabda* (1464 AD). My destiny is full of expeditions."

The meeting ended, and Gajapati was delighted. He left the hall and entered the palace.

With all these mind-blowing achievements, the mind of the great Gajapati was humbled by the events he had heard at Gajapati Castle of Koleru. A non-Odia General's daughter sacrificed her life to save the secret castle of Odisha, shed commotions in his mind, and a few drops of tears rolled down his face in memory of her and thousands of dedicated soldiers of Gajapati Forces.

Parshuram Vijay Melodrama

Gajapati Kapilendra Deva had declared himself the 'Raut' or servant of Lord Jagannath. In honour of his young brother, Veer Narendra Deva, he undertook the renovation of the Narendra Lake, a significant project. With fourteen nephews, each Ghat of the lake was named after them, leaving a lasting legacy. This renovation of Narendra Lake played crucial role in facilitating the Chandan Festival.

Gajapati Kapilendra Deva was deeply commited to safeguarding the boundaries of the Jagannath Temple. To enhance its security, he oversaw the construction of two significant walls: the *Kurma Prachira,* an inner wall and the the *Meghanada Prachira,* a sturdier outer wall made of stone. The temple premises had always been a vibrant centre of culture and root of Vaishnava religion. Under Gajapati Kapilendra Deva's patronage, the temple flourished as a hub for performing arts, including drama and Odissi dance. It served as a platform for cultural and artistic expression, enriching the lives of the people.

Cultural associations of Odisha and the servitors of *Srimandira* felt the expression of the firm will of the Gajapati. *Srimandira* management selected the Theatre staff. Puri has been a cultural hub for centuries and has abundant players. Several charge artists, Odishi dancers, speech editors, dramaturgists, and fight directors exist here. Dance Platforms or Natya Mandaps are invariably associated with the temple structure in Odisha. The temple has ample experience to stage any mythological drama of Hindu mythology and Sanskrit epics.

Puri Srimandira had been the seat of the culture of the Odia race. Any achiever exhibits their achievement here as a premier show. Dance groups, Singers, and orchestra groups of Odia songs have performed here on the expansive Grand Road during the Car Festival since antiquity. *Natya Mandaps* are integral parts of temples of Odisha in general, so any play has a greater sphere to be staged there with elite spectators. *Natya Mandap* of Puri Temple was the venue of Gajapati Kapilendra Deva's play of Parshurama Vijay.

ParshuramVijaya was to be staged on *Chandan Purnima*, the last day of Odia month Baisakha. The day was a mist of appropriate and auspicious with a full moon night. Gajapati Kapilendra Deva was the playwright, and the communicating language was both Sanskrit and Odia mixed. The duration of the play was one and a half hours.

Chandan Jatra

Chandan Jatra of Puri, starting on auspicious *Akshyaya Trutiya*, is a 21-day-long festival of Baisakh month at the height of summer heat. Sandalwood paste and water are components used to cool a person from the scorching heat of the Sun. Such cooling is in Chandan Jatra festival with a water trip of Lords in the Narendra Lake for pleasure. Mahalaxmi and Bhudevi, with the substitutes of Sri Jagannath, Rama Krishna, Lakshmi and Saraswati and five Shivas in special palanquins, move to the Lake of Narendra for a sacramental evening sail. This festive occasion attracts many pilgrims from all over India—the tourist spot crowds to a great extent.

For the successful casting of the play, *Parshurama Vijaya,* the director of the show, had the responsibility to rehearse it for at least two weeks. The enthusiastic director was rehearsing the play outside the temple. Members of the group gave the green signal to proceed. The play of *Parshurama Vijaya* is now in front of thousands of spectators in the Natya Mandap of *SriMandira*.

Coming to the main text of the treatise, Kshatriya King SahasrabahuKartaviryaArjun had the power of thousand arms. Sahasrabahu killed Jamadagni, a great sage and father of Parshurama, to get ownership of *Kamadhenu*, the divine cow. At that time, Parshurama was learning warfare lessons from Lord Shiva in the Kailash Mountains in the Himalayas. As soon as he completed his assignments, he returned home. A disciple of Jamadagni informed Parshurama of his father's death. Parshurama vowed to kill Sahasrabahu Kartavirya. Parshurama fought a great battle with Sahasrabahu, and he killed the evil king and freed the earth from the world of Kshyatriyas.

Lord Parshurama

Before the start of the play, the director of the space put forth a foreword: "His Highness Gajapati of Odisha wrote this play during his overloaded period.

It implies that his experience of the contemporary period has a significant role in the war scenes of this play. He must be observing one character as his ideal and executing his assignments. In all his appointments, he had a clear vision of a Hero who had superhuman powers. I must speak out; His Highness must have encountered many Kartaviryas in his Deccan expedition.

"Lord Parshurama of the Puranic period has impressed him. Parshurama was a courageous person with an axe with supernatural powers as his weapon. Lord Parshurama was the most influential person on earth. His axe had four cutting edges of his axe. "

Now I welcome all the spectators here to enjoy the play. I thank Rain God, Indradev, for favouring us with a perfect moonlit night with a clear sky and cool breeze from the sea.

This play produced a wave of warmth in the hearts of the spectators. In the Exposition of the Play, an Odissi dance that mimicked a war setting was displayed to arouse interest among the spectators. Each spectator was eager to see the appearance of Lord Parshurama. But the hospitality offered to great Emperor Kartavirya by the Sage Jamadagni was highly impressive; suddenly, his *Ashrama* could be hospitable to the tremendous force accompanying the Emperor satisfactorily.

The Emperor was astonished by the capacity

of Sage Jamadagni and enquired about the ability to satisfy such a crowd at the unprecedented hour. He came to know the divine cow, Kamadhenu and took no time to carry away Kamdhenu and, in the process, killed Jamadagni.

Parshurama, on his return from the Himalayas, received the information and charged the Emperor for killing his father and confiscating *Kamadhenu*. The mighty Kartavirya did not care for his reaction and sent a vast military to control him, But the solitary warrior, Parshurama, massacred the colossal army. Then there was the confrontation of the Kartavirya with Parshurama.

The crowd enjoyed every scene. The slicing of nine hundred ninety-eight hands of thousand armed Kartavirjya was the most memorable scene of the night.

Most importantly, Gajapati Kapilendra Deva witnessed the play and was very satisfied with the artists' costumes, direction and performance. The director invited His Highness, the playwright, to the dais for comments. He emerged from among the spectators in a civil dress and was invited to the stage.

The director stated, "Your Honour, the audience is eagerly waiting to see you on the dais as the playwright. The gesture of the audience is highly satisfactory. Even then, your epic *ParshuramaVijaya* must have taken its current shape with something in your mind, your Majesty. The decent assessment of the characters of this play reveals your spectacular histrionic talent.

The theme of the play dumbfounded the audience. We invite Your Highness to see how much we have been successful in expressing the role as per the playwright's expectations."

Gajapati came to the centre of the stage. The candle bearers came closer to him so that he could be distinctly visible to the audience, sitting tight even if the show had appropriately ended. The expression of the Gajapati was very much joyful and satisfied. He looked like the actor Parshurama in the play. His expression was a sign of rage. His facial glare designated the strength of a thousand lions. Everybody appreciated him as if the Parshurama was there revealing his mammoth physique, bow in the shoulder and an axe in hand, a raged Brahmin by Hindu caste but a *Kshyatriya* in action.

He started, "My dear fellowmen of Odisha, did you enjoy my play? It is all possible for latent human power within our body and mind. We cannot find any brave and capable warrior other than Parshuram. We have seen his confrontation with the mighty Emperor, Kartavirya Arjuna. Kartavirya Arjun had killed his father, Jamadagni, and forcibly taken away Kamadhenu. Parshuram single-handedly smashed Kartavir's massive army of seventeen *Akshauhinis*. When Kartavir arrived in his divine golden chariot, he was a mighty archer with a shooting capability of five hundred arrows at a time. But Parshuram damaged Kartavirya's bows, slew his horses and destroyed his chariot. Parshurama deflected the opponent's rocks and trees hurled at him and hacked off his thousand arms with an axe.

"Once we focus on our determination, no doubt it will succeed. Neighbours were infiltrating the motherland from all sides. I surrendered to Lord Jagannath as a disciple and fearlessly faced my enemies with all force and tact at my disposal. It was the crucial juncture. I ascended the throne, I had to amass the elephant force and channel them in the direct path as determined by Parshurama, and I have shown the results with 5 of the Sultanates at Malwa who were supporting the initial rebels, Jaunpur, who intermittently attacked our northern border, Bengal who had no warning for his attack on us, Delhi who organized a raid on Bahamani and us for treachery and inhumanity. We intend for a welfare state and have instructed my people in administration not to resort to atrocities and impose any authoritative rule. I am free to announce Odisha is our state, Odia is our mother-tongue, and Lord Jagannath is our State deity."

Ultimately, his facial expression returned to normal, smiling Kapilendra Deva; he started smiling at all spectators. It did not feel like Gajapati, but as if true Parshurama is standing there and convincing the spectators of the packed NatyaMandap, the

Chairperson is a character, and each can be as determined as Parshurama Bhagwan.

The speech of the Gajapati ended; the *Meghanada Prachira* had echoes of the inspirational voice of the Gajapati repeatedly to keep warming up the spirit of the dispersing audience.

Kapilendra Deva

A Disturbed Gajapati

The scriptures urge us to embrace the stage of *Vanaprastha*, the third stage of the *varnashrama* life system, as they reach the advanced age. During this phase, one is encouraged to relinquish household responsibilities, assume an advisory role, and gradually withdraw from worldly affairs. It is time to turn one's focus toward seeking God for spiritual liberation. However, there was a notable exception in the case of the formidable great conquerer, Sri-Sri-Sri-Gajapati-Gaudeswar-Nabakoti-Karnata-Kalabargeswar-Kapilendra Deva, who, at the age of eighty, defied the conventional wisdom.

Under Kapilendra's rule, the vast territory of Odisha had expanded significantly, stretching from the Ganges to Godavari and even much beyond. It reached as far as the Setubandha, the bridge connecting Bharatavarsha (the Indian subcontinent) and Sri Lanka, famously constructed by Lord Sri Rama during Ramayan Era. This period witnessed a remarkable improvement in the living standards of the Odias, and the entire province of Odisha, under the reign of the Gajapati Empire, shone with opulence.

The hostile neighbours surrounding the empire had ceased their attempts to assess the strength of its cavalry and elephantry forces. They had come to recognise the empire's formidable power and had submitted in resignation. Gajapati *Maudamani*, the greatest Gajapati, deservedly received admiration for his audacious expansion of the empire's boundaries. His courage and determination were unparalleled, making him a figure of historical significance.

In that long spell of a thirty-year reign, Kapilendra Deva never did bother about anyone's comments. He surrendered all his desires himself at Lord Jagannath's feet. He has only one vow, not to allow anyone to own even an inch of the soil of Odisha that he had gained by now. He longed for His blessings to acquire and annex all the extensive coastal tracts of Kalinga Sagara, the vast coast facilitating Odisha to garner commercial riches, build an Odisha, green and boundless, and create an example of an ideal culture.

But what is going on this day?

An unbelievable story was doing the rounds! In his dear queen's dream, the Supreme Lord had revealed that he should crown Queen Parvati's son Purushottama as his successor. None in the Jagannath temple could accept this. Some even spitefully said, "yea, why not Gajapati himself had got the throne that way! He will repeat the same thing now, also! Where has our mighty warrior Hamvira Deva gone? In his father's absence, he, a crown prince, went on conquering all the kingdoms to the South of Odisha. He is the worthiest son of the king. Strange that Lord Jagannath decreed in the dream to hand over the kingdom to the son of a frivolous queen instead of making the crown prince its anointed protector!"

Kapilendra Deva was in deep remorse. In the name of Jagannath, he had estranged *Matta* Bhanudev even when he was alive and usurped the throne of Odisha with his military power. *Matta* Bhanudev, too, had settled at Gudari for years and seen Kapilendra Deva's rule since the commencement of *Kapilabda*, the calendar in circulation in the name of Kapilendra Deva. The fathomless sorrow and grief Bhanudev had felt in his last days, won't he Kapilendra Deva suffer at least a modicum of it? The sprawling empire of the Ganga dynasty faced a hopeless smashing!

Well, let bygones be bygones.

Those jabs of pain and remorse, although after so long a time, were pressing him today from all sides. It is a fact that he has deprived the eldest prince of his due. It is a fact that Lord Sri Rama in Ramayana crowned Bharata and didn't himself be the king. Only Lord Jagannath knows who and why in the Barabati palace at Cuttack, someone played the role of Manthara, the hump-backed ill-natured lady in Ramayana. That ruthless decision was like an ominous comet for

Odisha; of course, King Dasaratha's queen Kaikeyi was comparable to Kapilendra Deva's slave queen Parvati. This Brahmin lady, a devotee of Jagannath, was extraordinarily charming, and Kapilendra Deva had used her a lot for his pleasure in his military expeditions. She became an eyesore for the eldest queen and other queens because of the king's love for an enslaved woman. However, Parvati never lost herself in narcissistic self-love. Her maidservant made her up and also scripted every piece of her conversation with others. Parvati's female cohorts practically tried like Kaikeyi and took assurance from the king to crown her son Purushottama soon after his birth.

The observers were watchful. All of Gajapati's sons were aspirants for the throne since they were princes of Odisha. The then society wanted Prince Hamvira Deva to ascend the throne per the rule of right primogeniture. In recent decades, he had proved his courage in his war expeditions in the Deccan. But at last, the father took a strange decision like a dictator. Gajapati Kapilendra Deva had taken the one-sided decision to make Purushottama the next Gajapati by hook or by crook, even though Purushottama had no war experience or capability in any other field. He certainly had the blessings of Lord Jagannath; he had named him Jagannath only because Lord Jagannath is otherwise called Lord Purushottam.

Hamvira Dev looked more challenging like Ramachandra of the Ramayana. He opposed it vehemently. It was a great insult to the prince, to the motherland. He failed to understand why his father practically disowned him. His mother, the eldest queen of Kapilendra Deva, could not meet Hamvira Dev either. The regent queen was mute to her husband's nasty politics and deceitful diplomacy. It resembled the infamous dice play in Mahabharata. And Hamvira Deva's virtuous son Dakshineswar has now been posted as the Parichha of Kondavidu. Kapilendra Deva felt as if the earth was slipping from under his feet. It was not merely a fistful of clay but his eldest son, who had been more sinned against than sinning. He could painstakingly build the vast empire brick by brick. It could treble itself in the area after he annexed the southern territories. And till this happened, it was a crumbling empire that the last Ganga king had left for him. The Gajapati was going to lose his mental balance. When the kingdom was tottering, the Gajapati had by his side Antarang Mahapatra or an officer who was also his closest confidant.

One must be the closest to the Emperor from the band of courtiers and ministers in the administration of the Gajapati kingdom. From the day Kapilendra Deva established himself as the Gajapati, his most intimate companion was Antarang Mahapatra, his secretary. His full name was Uchhabaa Bairiganjana. He and his family had endeared themselves to the Odisha king from his forefathers' days. Professionally too, Antarang Mahapatra was Kapilendra Deva's closest minion.

Uchhabaa observed Gajapati was not stable; his face looked sullen and worried. He found no peace in the palace. He led him gently to the armchair. Gajapati was mum, no word on his lips.

"The time has come, Uchhabaa, the time has come," he whispered, "The time has come for the atonement of sin. Perhaps my days are numbered, and my life in the lap of Odisha is running out!"

Uchhabaa Bairiganjana was more than just an official. His family has been the eyewitness of administrative and family affairs of the royal line for generations so far as the Utkal-Kalinga kings were concerned. His father and grandfather were also Mahapatras of the Ganga kings, and they were very conversant with the undercurrent of every affair and all transactions of royal administration. Uchhabaa Bairiganjana was the same age as the Gajapati Kapilendra Deva, so that he could read his mind well.

Uchhabaa realized that a disaster akin to a severe earthquake had recently struck Barabati Castle at Bidanasi Cuttack, which had seriously discomposed the royal family. When the impossible is a fact before us, it creates havoc. The incomparable Gajapati of Odisha has been inflicted with deep wounds and is writhing in pain. He is in the severest mental distress. His days of physical prowess as an army General on the battlefield and getting the highest accolades for his military exploits have passed. Today in this senile stage of life, he is burdened with a disturbed life.

Who knew that Kapila Raut one day would accomplish the impossible with his muscle power even though he was not a royal scion? The alien Reddy forces captured Kalinga or Odisha while its last Ganga king was engaged in fruitless battles on the south border. On its crumbling frontiers, he is today destitute amid plenty. The then courtiers, Mahapatras and Administrators felt the feebleness of their motherland, its leaderless anarchy, and its lack of unifying and expanding spirit. Ganga power had weakened and had reached the stage of being wiped out forever. Precisely at this time did Kapilendra Raut appear to the elite class in Odisha as a flaming torch because of his army deployment and military operation skills. At that time, he was visible as the only army General. The Unseen Power was concerned for the life of Odias as it was concerned for liberating the ultimate symbol of Odisha's life and culture, Lord Jagannath, from the ignominy of being defeated by the idol-smashing Muslim bandits. The Odia mindset always attributed its life and prosperity to the blessings of the Lord. It saw the protective hand of the Lord whenever it faced danger.

Just then, everyone noticed General Kapilendra. He was an ambitious military specialist, a warrior who held his head high and showed courage. He inspired such loyalty in his men that they'd follow him anywhere, if necessary. He is the close confidant of Ganga king *Matta* Bhanudev with an astute understanding of royal affairs. Kapilendra himself was in deep thought as to why the Ganga king kept the kingdom in the dark for months when he got stuck in those fruitless battles. Instead, he could have commanded him for assistance. Why are the breeding puzzles on the frontiers?

A gifted Mahapatra put forth a proposal to Kapilendra Deva secretly. He had a question about the future of the dying Ganga rule. His voice was firm with a hidden resolve, "Speak up, valiant Kapilendra, put forth your view. The courtiers and ministers of Odisha want Odia soldiers to fight elegantly and gracefully in battles and be happy with Odia's official administration. They don't want the royal power to be feeble enough to remain helpless along the border for months and finally surrender to the enemy. Will the enemy retreat from the border if we bow down before them?"

One by one, many courtiers and ministers were also prompting General Kapilendra with the same kind of suggestion. The Ganga king is subdued and lacklustre. Reddy, an administrator of Rajamahendry, obliterated the image of Ganga King *Matta* Bhanudev through the conspiracy. Reddy was an agent appointed by the king of Vijayanagara of Karnata(k). The kingdom has lost hope, and there is a great suspicion that King *Matta* Bhanudev would return safely from the South. Won't he thrust farther into Rajamahendri and easily be trapped by Reddy? The south border of Odisha was caving in without resistance. So easy for the enemy!

The next day a messenger from the southern

border brought some sad news to the military council. It was that Simadri Forte had fallen to Bhima Reddy of Rajamahendry. Visakhapatnam, too, was occupied by Vijayanagara. All the courtiers, including ministers, administrators, and the chief custodian of Jagannath temple, assembled because of the danger. They were busy discussing what they would do for the coming days. Administration-in-charge Kapilendra Deva also was present. Then they all spoke in one voice, "General Kapilendra Rautray will sit on the throne of Odisha from tomorrow."

But Kapil was stunned. He was silent for a moment and then muttered." No, it's impossible. Kapilendra is the army General of the Ganga dynasty. His blood has the warmth of battles he had fought for the Gangaraj. He can never be a serpent in his lap."

Kapilendra Deva didn't support the proposal because he thought it was not straightforward. All the feudal chiefs of the empire were on the side of Ganga. There was every possibility that they together would defeat the new dispensation. They would declare war simultaneously, occupy Bidanasi Cuttack or will cut off all ties with central administration.

Kapilendra, the army General, was in deep thought. "What will I get you crown me without solving this problem? I am the General of the Army. How far is it right to be the ruler of the kingdom? It is a matter of great puzzle for me," he thought.

Without wasting more time, the Mukhya Kasinath Mahapatra interceded, "There is little possibility of *Matta* Bhanudev arriving here. In this case, let the inevitable happen. Our decision, therefore, is Kapilendra Raut should be in a hideout elsewhere, barring Cuttack and Puri, and will declare himself as the king of the whole territory and display his might and support base. The consequence will be that Bengal will stop its intrusions, and with it, Jaunpur independent Muslim Nawab, who is planning to attack Odisha, will recede."

He continued, "Let's be over with the crowning in secret at Papanasini Temple near Ekamra Kruttibash temple on Wednesday, that is, Kakada Dwitiya Shukla Chaturthi of the month of Shravan in the current Saka year 1357, and on 29th June, 1435 as per Christian calendar. The General will post the personnel of his private army for safety at strategic places, and the royal mission is to be carried out with utmost secrecy."

Kapilendra looked a little suspicious regarding that confidential action plan. Still, one could easily see his interest in the program, not so much for himself as for the empire's defence and restoring the dignity of Odisha. Protection of Utkal art and sculpture and Lord Jagannath from destructive forces was the need of the hour. Above all, the General had his choicest ambitions for his motherland.

Of course, he could sense that usurping the throne would never let Gangas or its successors excuse him. *Matta* Bhanudev has happily adopted him as his son because of his military skill. But, for that matter, why should he accept him as his father? As a skilful General, he could never be confident about Bhanudev. The same Ganga kings had once attacked Banga and wrecked and ruined it. King Narasimha Deva didn't ever let them into Odisha.

On the other hand, he could gain plenty of wealth from victory on Lakhnauti and Champa. Sad that *Matta* Bhanudev proved incompetent, with no morality and no courage. Well, what else an effeminate king would be?

Coronation of Kapilendra was done secretly with the vow to serve his subjects, kingdom, cows and Brahmins. *Matt*a Bhanudev never returned to Barabati, but his relatives, three feudal chiefs, became enemies with Kapilendra Deva. They were chiefs of the feudatories Khemundi, Nandapur and Odadi near Simadri. They were the blood relations of his forefathers but were more desirous of acquiring the unstable imperial crown than of their loyalty to *Matta* Bhanudev. They had another irresistible desire to usurp the throne because there was no legitimate heir to Bhanudev. But Kapilendra Deva ended all that. Leave alone their support, the subordinate vassal kings would not even pay the taxes and would always oppose him. They would publicly narrate how Kapilendra Deva had ascended the throne by adopting deceitful ways. They would paint it before the people as treachery to Lord

Jagannath's devotee *Matta* Bhanudev and tell them it was nothing but hitting Purushottama with a hatchet.

Khemundi Rivals

Kapilendra Deva felt as if the ground under his feet was sinking. Lord Jagannath was staring at him in a fury, for he was causing turmoil in a land of peace.

All those random thoughts of Uchhabaa Mahapatra halted when he recalled Gajapati's words on impending danger. Indeed Kapilendra Deva was cowering inside himself after being declared king of Kalinga. But thank Lord, the courage in his psyche rose splendidly like the rising morning Sun.

He felt bold. He resolved: Kapilendra Deva will never let Kalinga-Utkal be wounded at heart. Mother Odisha will help him if he works for the motherland. With the blessings of the goddess, if one grows, all obstacles will vanish. The restlessness in Kapilendra Deva subsided at these thoughts.

A couple of Ganga feudal families cleared out like dark clouds blown away by the wind leaving nothing behind. Let the three southern feudatories not pay the taxes. But none has the muscle to defeat the General of the Kalinga army individually, that too, on his native land. He is the descendant of a Kshatriya clan. He is quite adept in both dynastic and administrative affairs. The undercover operation ending in accession to the throne will prevent ridicule in a rumour-prone place like Puri. The other story was that a royal elephant poured water from the golden pot anointing a commoner like Kapilendra as Gajapati, and his childhood friend became his closest confidant. Of course, this was folklore and could never be true.

Be it as it may, they admitted that Kapilendra Deva was their dearest king. Apart from many supporters of the Ganga King, those jealous and vociferous fans of Ganga King were cursing his incredible luck. Be it the incident of a cobra spreading its hood on Kapilendra Deva's head or Bhanudev calling Kapilendra his foster child; both were the dawn of good fortune.

Kapilendra Deva came to realize that he was losing mental composure. Before he could focus his mind on his physical strength, he muttered, "Erasing his identity was good. Another thing is that my friend Kasia has been dragged firmly into the rumour. Outside this slander and hidden from these slanderers is Kasinath Mahapatra, the kingdom's Chief Minister, who could do everything to see Kapilendra Deva on the royal robes for Odisha. The same Kasinath Mahapatra is the *Kasia* of the "Kasia-Kapila rumour wrongly believed by Odias. .

Kapilendra Deva knelt before the Jagannath idol and mumbled, "Lord, give me infinite moral courage. I swear before you, Lord, I shall achieve all my goals. This vast kingdom, along with you, will remain my greatest concern. Odisha will get all-around progress, growth in her wealth, restoration of her dignity."

And there followed thirty-three years of Kapilendra Deva's reign for all to see. He changed the course of the history of Odisha. Rising from the military rank of one of the greatest generals, he created a vast kingdom that stretched from the Ganges to the southern end of India. No other name but only "Odisha" could apply to this extensive tract. He used his large number of native elephants to form the mammoth elephantry. He had a charismatic and sensible personality; the Gajapati army with native Paikas was extremely loyal, believing him throughout all hardships. He was highly ambitious. It was unique in contemporary Bharatavarsha.

Odia could be the language of Odisha, of the royal court and in all other fields. Looking at Sarala Mahabharata, the lone star in Odia literary heaven, one must agree that the Odia language had the potential to represent Odisha in all respects. It amply justified

Gajapati's intentions to make Odia the language of his motherland. Gajapati Kapilendra Deva had achieved all his cherished goals, usually the world expected of him. The unrivalled Gajapati-Gaudeshwar-Karnatakala-Bargeswar staunchly believed in Lord Jagannath, the Lord of the universe.

But alas, Gajapati felt helpless at the end part of his life! He thought his family was a temple of trust, but those members rebelled against him. Kapilendra Deva had appointed them as Parichcha or supervisors. He deployed massive armies to assist them. Yet they didn't submit to his decision to obey the Lord's decree even though no one would think of disregarding God's Will, let alone ignore it. These princes do not accept the order that Lord Jagannath has passed Himself! Lord Jagannath Himself has ordained who would succeed him, and the princes could not receive it!

Gajapati was disconsolate. A confidential report had come that Vijayanagara trespassed on the southern border of Odisha. Gajapati looked much more agitated this time. However, whatever happened to his family, he would not let it distract him from his duty of protecting his motherland. He would not allow even an inch of land away from the monumental Odisha Rashtra.

Old Gajapati was confounded, brooding over why the Lord had tricked him. He was mused the next moment by divine sight, which is more mystical than human perception. How could anybody disregard who would be chosen as royal successor to the throne by Sri Jagannath?

But the dilemma still haunted Gajapati: the pressure of governance, family disturbances and social scandals. He felt as if all his military glory and prowess were draining away. He felt crushed under the worries.

"What shall I do?" he couldn't but whisper to Him anxiously, "Lord, thou help my inaction."

Gajapati today is pulled down by old age. He is saddened, his head resting on his trembling hands. Could it be that Hamvira Deva went against his father? He, too, has plenty of stakes in the Gajapati Empire. He is the supreme ruler of the whole southern region. And not that his son Dakshina Kapileswar Mahapatra has been appointed only as the Parichha of the mighty Kondavidu fort. In addition, he has taken to the maintenance of many Shiva and Vishnu temples and has defeated the anti-Odisha mindset of the rival Vijayanagara kingdom. He is such a consummate master of martial art that none could ever dare to intrude into the limits of his fort.

If my eldest son does not succeed to the throne, will he feel let down? He should understand why his father had made such a strange decision and why he had ignored his eldest son and other princes and chosen Purushottam as the successor.

The entire episode flashed in his mind. Winter

had set in. Harvesting was going to be over. It had been so many days since the nine varieties of dishes in Jagannath temple were ready. It had been scheduled before, on December 14, 1466, that Gajapati would tour the Purushottam Puri temple from the palace at Barabati Cuttack with family to perform some religious rituals. As it had been during the last five times, this tour was to convey to Lord Jagannath the vast extent of victories and acquisition of honour. It was to beg the Lord to bless him with His decree on a particular issue: Purushottam Jagannath's divine view on succession to Gajapati, to know who He would choose as his heir to the throne.

Lord Jagannath is the supremely impartial divinity. He is the supreme soul who none can question. Odias have always honoured His decree. They all have unwavering faith in His ways that see no distinction between rich and poor, the ruler and the ruled. In this Odisha Empire, anyone who offers evidence, even in a village court adjudicating a case, and does so by invoking the name of the Lord, such evidence is accepted as accurate. Any other information was of secondary value. There are a large number of antecedences to prove it.

Lord Jagannath alone has set many examples of pure justice in the past. As the story goes over, the worshipping of the Lord is with the hymns of the Jaydev's Gita-Govinda. Once King Narasimha Deva III wrote the version of Sri Gita-Govinda. Controversy arose regarding the preferred one by the deity. Given the chance to select, Lord Jagannath chose the version of Jayadev as superior, who was acknowledged far and wide as the greatest poet and devotee of Lord Krishna. The Gajapati Empire's supreme ruler Kapilendra Deva came to the Lord with a similar controversy. Time itself awaits the announcement of one of the conclusive proclamations by Gajapati. Not that the future of the Gajapati family depended on it. It could be suicidal if internal squabbles are visible to the Muslim kingdoms surrounding Odisha.

"Why did he think of Purushottam, the youngest child to sit on the throne? The idea itself was eating into his heart. Of course, Prince Hamvira never claimed the throne. Can Purushottam's mother use this to fulfil her desire to crown him? She has earned her worth by fully dedicating herself to caring for him, although countless servants and well-wishers have also taken up this duty….Have I lost my mind at this ripe age?" he mused.

Those words kept echoing in his mind. "My Purushottama alone will be the second Gajapati of Odisha." His thoughts didn't stop. Queen Parvati had repeatedly told me that all human qualities were with Purushottam and all evil rates were with Hamvira Deva, thus poisoning my mind in the Barabati palace. Well, no use blaming Parvati Devi. Rather than a dark-skinned companion of hers who is more evil-minded than Manthara of Ramayana. She coaxed me with her sweet words and was able to separate me from my worthy son.

He recalled that occasion when he had been to the shrine of Jagannath. There was a huge crowd waiting for him. When the royal entourage arrived, they rushed to the temple in one wave. They knew that His Excellency Gajapati Kapilendra Deva would unfailingly seek His permission whenever he wanted to move outside Odisha and do the same again in return. Lord's blessing was mandatory for any Royal work. The time when he returned from victory over the kingdom of Gauda, he came here to the temple of Lord Jagannath to assume the title of Gaudeshwar. And then this was inscribed on the temple wall. The same thing was common in many conquests, Karnat, Kalabarga etc., many such entitlements and inscriptions.

But now, that uninterrupted series of victories had become the story of the past. Why has Gajapati brought with him the whole of his family to Jagannath instead of those great warriors?

His mind veered to his declining age. He was eighty-plus. The eldest child Hamvira Deva was fifty-two, younger son Purushottam, was forty-five. Even Hamvira Deva's son and his grandson Kapileswar was twenty-four!

The eldest queen and the two princes were walking in a line. On the way, their eyes fell on the Kurumapacheri or turtle-shaped wall and the

Meghanada wall or sky-kissing outer wall of the palace he had built around the temples. The younger queen Parvati Devi was striding before the eldest queen.

The Emperor kept moving forward with the Lord in his mind. Beside him were the two sons. The Royal family was moving with several young family members behind him for a holy visit to the deity. Lord Jagannath Himself has summoned Kapilendra Deva and his family to announce His commandment. Even after ten years, who should be the heir to the Gajapati family needed to be clarified. Gajapati must not free himself from Odisha's administrative and military responsibilities. Even this third or the vanaprastha phase of life might be the last life span. When a man should lead the life of a hermit in a forest, he would face many challenges.

The people of Odisha had already learned that Gajapati was by then an older man and wished to lead a retired life in the forest because he had done his duty of founding the Suryavamsa dynasty and building the Gajapati Empire. But for some time, the Gajapati family had been beset with the succession problem that could reach the public domain. His eldest son Hamvira Deva was the ultimate Kshatriya and superb army General who caused havoc with his onslaughts on the Bahamani Muslim kingdom in the South and snatched the southern parts of the realm from Muslim control. The name of Hamvira Deva could terrify every prince and army general ruling over the southern kingdoms from Rajamahendri to Setubandha. The kingdom of Odisha must go to him, and the subjects would rest contented. The future of Odisha would be bright in all fields of military strength, agricultural production and cultural renaissance.

"Was he wilful and ruthless in refusing his elder son his due?"

Kapilendra Deva was startled at the thought.

His subjects were at a loss as to why Kapilendra Deva, the guardian that he was, could keep this vital decision a secret. If there was one man who always had his way and listened to none, he is Kapilendra Deva. Who could advise him? There were a host of officials in the position of Ministers and Mahapatras. They are all executive officers. But can any of them show him the right way with his advice? Well, sixteen senior Parts and other royal officials resided near the palace at Bidanasi Cuttack to aid and advise him collectively on being invited when such an occasion arises. However, Kapilendra Deva is highly self-willed. He decides his course. He did not care a hoot for social conventions and the rule of primogeniture. Although he knew the law, he wanted to subvert it!

The whole issue was a considerable question unsolved to date. If there was anyone who could raise the matter before the Emperor, it was the court official Kasinath Mahapatra. Still, in such a case, he could only do so in kingdom affairs, not the king's family matters.

The subjects also fondly accepted him as a benevolent dictator. He had an uncanny felicity in speech act and an infinite ability to work out his will. He never said," It is impossible," no matter howsoever impossible an assignment looked. They believe his tenacity will make him write a letter even to god Indra if there is no rain! Who can say "no' to such a man's command? Gajapati looked dejected.

He was dressed in a golden yellow fit-out, and the upper part of his body was adorned with ivory-coloured apparel of finest silk. Gold ornaments around his neck radiated their precious appearance befitting the ceremonial occasion. He started from the temple's main gate, the *lion's gate*. He was walking to the sanctum sanctorum, called the *Garbhagruha*. The Gajapati walked inside with Hamvira Deva on his right side and Purushottam on the left, and all the other princes formed a single line, one after the other. A tiny column of whirlwind was rolling stealthily above the gigantic outer wall of the palace. The whirlwind passed across the royal visitors. Unfortunately, the apparel worn on Gajapati's shoulders fluttered and slipped to the right in the wind. Hamvira Deva was relatively unresponsive, as if he did not see it. He watched all this but didn't touch it. But Purushottam quickly moved to the right, got the falling apparel and placed it gracefully on his father's shoulders.

With a grim look, a side-long glance at Hamvira Deva's displeasure was the feeling briefly expressed on the face of Gajapati. Jagannath was the living God. Manifestation of the Lord has since time immemorial. Instinctively he could know that. He said to himself, "Lord has evidenced his revelations…..".

The entourage of Patras and Ministers following him couldn't guess the mystery of the king's wind-swept scarf. The Gajapati suffused his emotions in deep devotion abruptly. He then dissolved in the divine frenzy. He raised both his hands in complete submission to Him. His first appearance with his Lord was when he fully surrendered to Him. He had come six years ago with loads of gems and jewels to adorn the Lord in gold. He could establish himself as Kapilendra-Raut, the most outstanding servant of the Lord. But this day for him was the day of total surrender.

The crowd there applauded to raise the atmosphere to a higher energy level.

Gajapati retrieved all his past events. The scene swam into his memory. "It was the year of my accession to the throne," he mused, "I had stepped into this temple one day with much hope. I decided to repeal many obsolete laws of governance. I got them proclaimed in the temple premises itself, "I withdraw from today, tax on salt and shell." Even now, I hear the loud applause from each one present here, Kanhei Santra, Gopinath Mangaraj, Beleswar Praharaj and others.

It was a day in my 15th year of rule - the incident of conquering Mallikarjunakonda or Srisaila in the South. The Odisha army captured the nine forts, one after the other. And thanks to the Lord, that too without any bloodshed. I had presented my Lord with a *Pundarika Gopa* saree and arranged the prettiest damsels to serve as *devadasis* who would prayerfully dance in His presence to amuse Him. For convenience, I stressed that temple services to be regular and continuous. That's the year when new things happen. The new additional titles were echoing in the temple bells. *Nabakoti-Karnat-Kalbargeswar* was a new addition to Sri Sri (108 times) and Gaudeswar. Since then, before every time he wielded the wand, the Chamberlain or Pratihar would chant all these titles, including the required number of Sri's.

In the next decade, with the expansion of the southern boundary of Odisha came copious amounts of wealth from conquests. The Minister in charge of treasury at Simadri Fort sent sixteen elephant loads of precious metals obtained after the victory over South to Lord Jagannath. It was the victory of the Lord, not was it the victory of the Gajapati military forces. It was that of the unique and omnipotent doer of all things, Lord Jagannath. The idols of Jagannath temple were adorned gracefully with another one hundred and thirty-eight types of golden ornaments on Bada Ekadasi, the eleventh lunar day in the month of Kartika celebrated in Puri. And that was the beginning of the Lord's *Sunabesha*, a fully ornament-clad appearance.

"In this ceremony, adorning the Lord with golden jewels is customary. *Sunabesh* ceremony is not symbolic of the Lord's wealth. It signifies the riches of Odisha and the Odia psyche."

Tears rolled down his cheeks spontaneously. None could make out why. Such a feeling of Kapilendra Deva showing the finest sensitivity stunned all the officials. None of them could fathom how the General of so many battles, a tough and emotionally hardened Gajapati, could be drowned in the bottomless depths of devotion to the Lord, losing his rugged attitude altogether. His heart never melted, not even at the gory sight of mountains of dead Bahamani soldiers. He had never been as much compassionate as Ashok, the Maurya emperor. Today why could he be so much tearful? He felt he had entered into a complicated problem. He has come to the Jagannath temple to offload his burden on the deity for a solution.

Last year's proclamation for Jagannath flashed in his mind, "All my jewellery from today belongs to Jagannath." He had also announced that he would dissolve his being at the lotus feet of the Lord.

He had an irresistible urge to get *darshan*, to bow in the presence of the Lord prayerfully. But his heart was full of pain - no response from Jagannath. No sign from Him about His decree, Was all that dream matter before not true? Is it that I had not rightly interpreted the dream? Is it that he had not seen the vision himself and had acted on someone else's dream to determine his successor to the throne in the name of Lord Jagannath?

In his old age, his competent queen Parvati only was his constant companion. She was the wisest concubine queen of Kapilendra Deva. She was born into a Brahmin family. She deserved the position of the king's confidant by her sharp wit. She was Gajapati's closest adviser. That Kapilendra who listened to none in his youth, if now listens to anyone, it is Parvati. She has advised him pretty long all his life. The greatest thing she did was to bear his child Purushottam. At birth, she had whispered to him that he was Jagannath's blessing and should be named Purushottam. She had assured him that he would prove the worth of such a name in his life. Why can't he be the second Gajapati?

That's all a past story. Some wicked lady in the family had infected his bond with Parvati. Parvati was a pretty woman. It isn't easy to guess who and how somebody tied Parvati to him when he grew from strength to strength in his early life as Kapila Raut, the army General and a powerful and rising Kshatriya hero. Kapila could not have fallen for a Brahmin girl. He then had more onerous responsibilities, like the security of the kingdom. In addition to this, the Odia militia was in complete disarray. For generations, it had taken substandard recruits. Ganga king Narasimha Deva's fearful army had declined because the soldiers had forgotten that fighting spirit during the following ages of two centuries. When foot soldiers fail to resist risking their life, the army is bound to degenerate. This untold pain was eating into Kapil Raut's heart. He was trying to find a way out without asking anyone for advice and assistance.

Taking advantage of his agonizing preoccupations, a supplier of sorts told him in private that in an Odia woman, there is a paragon of beauty. He goaded him, saying anybody may kidnap her anytime, and she needs security. In that period of hectic activity and despite his unwillingness, he absent-mindedly imagined her to be like a daughter to his parents. Soon Parvati's bewitching beauty won him over, and all those caste obstacles faded from his mind. He forgot he was married and had his wife and child, Hamvira Deva.

Of all the children of a king, the child of the eldest queen, from his childhood, hopes to be the prince chosen for the throne. When Kapila Raut was invested with legal power after being anointed in Ekamra Kruttibash temple, an explosion-like incident occurred in his own family. Within a few months of Kapilendra's secret accession, Gopinath Mahapatra, the in-charge of Barabati, invited Kapilendra, the secretly anointed king of Odisha. It was a cordial invitation to shift him from his General's quarters to the palace. Before the Raut family could fully relish the joy of settling in the castle and his wife could feel at home with the new place, Parvati had taken full possession of the palace from her house provided by Kapilendra Deva.

By the time Hamvira Deva was twenty-five when his father was the Emperor. But Hamvira Deva had achieved his father's goal before that and proved his bravery. Kapil Raut had been successful in siring an Odia warrior stronger than himself. In the meanwhile, the same Hamvira Deva had also become his chief functionary. However, Hamvira Deva was an ordinary cavalryman when Odisha's unknown ministers and well-wishers advised them to crown his father as king of Odisha.

Often Hamvira Deva would enjoy riding to distant places on some confidential kingdom work. He had tremendous faith in his achievements and his works. None could see him too much immersed in devotion for any god or disrespecting the Lord. He was grateful to him because He had given him the strength to do the impossible. He didn't want anything more than His blessings. He recollected how he could do the unthinkable to raise the honour of Odisha. Still, he has extended its boundary farther and farther, conquering the kingdoms along its borders.

Who can hit and break the tenacity of such an all-conquering hero? For long, none has dared advise Kapilendra Deva, the father of Odisha. In such a scenario, why should anyone think of opposing his will? Of course, only the Lord can make it possible to endear the crowning of the younger prince to the subjects. Kapilendra was in deep thought on this problem. Well, the Lord alone could show the way.

He was looking for an alternative too. If Purushottam were not the king, family life would be hell. Ten years had passed; he could not decide whom to choose for the throne. Reliance on the Lord's revelation could settle the issue. Since it is an oracular pronouncement, no one can oppose it. He must be decisive in the face of all such stumbling blocks.

"He had given the final word to Parvati only last night that Purushottam would succeed him. He will be the second Gajapati of Odisha," he heard himself saying.

At last, the announcement was made in the Jagannath temple only.

It stupefied them for a moment. And they said, "Alas, Hamvira! Poor Hamvira Deva!"

Then and there, the turmoil in his heart started: No more strength I have, Lord, help me out of the misery, his soul cried. Am I not indeed pushing my newly built Odisha empire into chaos?"

I have it to you, my Lord!

Gajapati had conquered all the territory around Odisha, thus enlarging it three times f its former size. Still, at the sunset of his life, due to family problems, his act of giving the throne to the youngest son instead of his eldest and announcing that Lord Jagannath had revealed in his dream to do so stunned the whole of the then Odisha. How could the Gajapati, the Lord of justice, the most eminent son of Odisha, and the patron of Odia language and culture, transgress the code of natural justice? His own heart revolted at this thought. He had left Barabati for the Krishna river banks. Saluva Narasimha of the Vijayanagara kingdom was recapturing the far-off Kaveri banks. This recapture was forcing him to be quick. Vijayanagara forces are silent so far, murmuring, perhaps a matter to defy him. On this side, Kapilendra Deva had lost interest in reigning any longer. Did he have the strength to go on campaigns? Moreover, his mind was full of gloom over the decade-long failure to choose an heir.

"The Lord didn't come to my help!" Gajapati was thinking.

"My eldest son Hamvira Deva, the first devotee of the Lord, left the palace on hearing the announcement. The eldest queen fainted the moment she heard it. The whole of the South is articulate in Hamvira Deva's praise. Perhaps, stung by this deep pain, Odisha as a whole is asking me one question. None has the guts to ask this question, but I feel it is in their hearts, and I can hear it. "At whose insinuation am I giving the throne to Purushottam when the eldest born is very much there?" My conscience urges me to say, "Jagannath has ordained it in my dream. Aha, that is my magic wand. Jagannath's name will solve all the problems. Then none will say a word against it. Everyone will accept it heartily.

"I have held my head high by doing the

impossible for my family and kingdom. But the highest ideal of it all is that I presented myself as the servant of Lord Purushottam. Of course, wealth and conquest of kingdoms do not hold much weight for God, yet when it comes to proving my ideal at the behest of the Lord, why don't my people accept it? One day, their devotion to Him will wipe out all their mental distress."

Remorse, caused by guilt, gripped him, and his soul writhed in severe turmoil, and he was in a dilemma, "Have I erred in choosing Purushottam as my heir? Did I pay no heed to my eldest child Hamvira Deva's rights?

"Why is there confusion in Gajapati's kingdom? Purushottam is a more excellent devotee of Jagannath. He is calm, quiet, talented and of exemplary character. I want him to be Jagannath's servant for this reason. Why should anyone object to it? Doesn't the Lord's ordination have that much weight? Had it not been in the divine scheme of things, had He not revealed the same in his dream?"

During the last thirty-two years, Hamvira Deva had not tasted what it felt to be like a Gajapati. He had been the Parichhas of such a giant-size fort, Kondavidu. And after selflessly working hard for so long, it would be unfair if he consented to let Purushottama ascend the throne of Odisha for its expansion and the spread of Jagannath culture.

"O Lord Jagannath, you are unjust to me. My family matters appear to me as a suicidal arrangement. My greatest weakness is the area of my motherland and my vow not to part with even the tiniest portion of my homeland to the hostile neighbours.

" Hamvira Deva has disappeared. Where has he gone? He has authority everywhere, whether Reddys or Bahamani, Udayagiri or Vijayanagara. The South is the balancing weight for today's Odishan Empire. If it loosens a bit, the empire will collapse in seconds. All my life-long labour will come to nought. I know the vast region from Ganga to Godavari is challenging to defend, rule, and keep intact on all sides. The gigantic elephant force is badly necessary. Only the elephant corps can ensure peace and stability there.

Unfortunately, there are not many Parichhas. Ruling over Odisha can continue only so long as Gajapati's eyes are on it. A little inattention, and there are instances of even Generals deserting the Gajapatis on the battlefield. Odia soldiers stake their lives in battles and always win. Yet, they would perform if given armament and military gear, and ten years of my reign just passed in doing this much. Be it the formidable armies of the Aira dynasty of Kumargiri, of the Kalinga war or the battle of Mahabharata, the fact is that warriors of all ages are born in the villages nestling at the foothills a stone's throw from the plain areas of the kingdom of Utkal. They were all the children of Odisha, the motherland of the brave.

They bow their head only to the motherland and defend it at any cost. Somebody must unite those leonine Kalinga soldiers and put them in the battle line before the enemy. That would be enough. The first Ganga king Chodaganga Deva showed such a feat when he ascended the throne of Odisha. The caravan of this saga rolled three generations down to King Narasimha Deva, and then the absence of strong leadership and the inspiring war drums let its wheel wedge slip loose. The Bahinipati title of this king inspired many Kshatriya and non-Kshatriya Generals. The military system occupied the whole of Odisha. The commanders adorned with various titles enhanced the spirit and strength of the military force. Artists and architects of Kalinga even built victory symbols like Konark, which were rare monuments in India. Architects, sculptors and artists matched the army with their skills as they built temples. Hence the Gangas are at the root of all those magnificent temples of Odisha.

The Lord's blessings are always with Odisha. Natural barriers extended on all sides of the kingdom to deter the outside enemy. Its terrain is bristled with forests and hills. The outstretched sea borders its plains. Besides, the hulking black elephants of Kalinga have kept the enemies at bay. Muslim forces had tried many times to thrust into this kingdom during the Ganga reign. Sometimes they would demand a couple of elephants from us and then retreat. But these Bengal Muslims have stared greedily at Odisha for the last two hundred years. If the king of Odisha went south, they would attempt to cross Mandaran to march up to the Lord's treasury at Puri.

This fear had many times made the Gajapati nervous. He had filled the coffers of the Lord in full public view. After such wide publicity, could this fact remain hidden from those marauders? He was in a dilemma. He had raised the gigantic outer wall around the Lord's temple, but one day, Jagannath Suna Besa, a golden embellishment ritual periodically performed, will invite danger. He could not overcome this fear.

"Had I enriched the treasury of the Lord in secret, Muslim rulers might not have known it." The next moment he dismissed it as something the Gajapati in him would never tolerate. "In our birthplace Odisha should we feign poverty for fear of the plunderers? No, Odisha's history and myth have shown it was impossible. We should rather drive out those Muslim forces from our soil and the neighbourhood. Let Odisha forever remain free from them." He cooled down a little at those thoughts.

His closest confidant Uchhaba arrived.

Anxiously Gajapati asked, "Uchhaba, how long it will take to leave Barabati?

"All are ready. There is an auspicious moment after one hour and a half. Six Manapatras, including me, will accompany you. The Manapatras will be on horseback guarding the rear, behind your chariot. If Your Excellency so wishes, you can take a bit of rest at short intervals. The Odisha military has arranged rest houses along our way. About one and a half hours to sunset, we shall reach the fort meant for our night sojourn. As Your Excellency relaxes, you would apprise the Manapatras of tomorrow's plans," he replied solemnly.

And still, Gajapati looked at him without a wink, anxiety writ large on his face. To reassure him, Uchhaba continued," I have selected and got only six Mahapatras ready as per your daily needs and to be in your service. *Sandhibigraha* Mahapatra Samaresh Bahubalendra will be with us. He is our war and treaty counsellor. Bahubalendra is the chief of the detachment for wars and treaties. He has knowledge and experience in domestic diplomacy, military strategy for border disputes, and mutual relationships between Odisha and its neighbours. In addition to this, if there is a breach of secret pacts between Odisha and Vijayanagara, if one of our men or even the king of Vijayanagara were to grind his axe because of our family quarrels, the responsibility to investigate and prevent the same rests in his hands only."

Gajapati looked inattentive. He turned to Uchhaba, expecting him to repeat something since he was absent-minded.

Uchhaba went on, "Bhīma Bhujabal is the defence department chief. As of today, Bangla and

Bihar look pitiable. Madhyadesh in the west also seems subdued. The news of uninterrupted Odisha victories in the South has created a commotion in the last decade. Odisha has proved its supremacy all over Bharatavarsha but also all over the world. The country rates Odisha as the most dreaded power. If Gajapati steps into the north beyond the Odisha boundary, all the Muslim forces of Delhi and Banaras will bolt into their land for self-protection. Well, that was Bhujabal's prediction too."

Bhujabal is ready to coordinate all the royal commands to ascertain the approximate expenses of our military expedition we are to incur on the protection of Parichchas and feudatories and the clearance of their dues." Uchhaba looked at Gajapati to read his mind.

He couldn't fathom whether Gajapati heard him or not. He doubted whether Gajapati kept silent knowingly or was heedless.

He implored, "My Lord, I beg your pardon. Shall we include War and Treaty Minister (*Sandhibigraha* Mahapata) and Defence Minister (*Pratirakshya* Mahapatra) in the team survey of the South?"

Gajapati replied promptly, 'They will come with us as you have suggested."

Uchhaba felt relieved. He felt assured that Gajapati was attentive. He pretended he wasn't and resumed, "Another bigraha will accompany.

The latter is the doorkeeper, Tribikram Mukut. His designation is Thau-dwara Pariksha. He has the power to decide prayer rituals and all temple matters. Odisha will always be ahead in the number of devout subjects. Our kingdom worships gods and goddesses and is the worshipper of divine power. But the Vijayanagara ruler paints the opposite and covertly spreads spiteful fiction such as "Saluva Narasimha is tarnishing the devout soul of Odisha." Tamils denounce *"galabhaiodiyara"* The touts of SaulvaNarasimha are spreading the rumour that Odisha has failed to maintain the temples of all captured kingdoms for years, leaving their deities unworshipped. These touts in Tamil Nadu defame Odisha calling it *"galabhaiodiyara"*, and in this way, build up Vijayanagara fame. If we appoint one Mahapatra in that region as the counsellor to the Parichhas, we can prevent such means and nasty propaganda of Vijayanagara against us.

Still, Gajapati sat blankly as if he did not listen to anything.

Antaranga again pursued, "Two Pujak Mahapatras will also accompany us from Puri."

This time Gajapati was startled. It seemed as if he was looking for the blessings of Jagannath. In his ripe old age, the Gajapati should desire His Company to prove his devotion to Him. He turned to Uchhaba. His expression on the face changed. He was all attentive.

Taking the cue, Uchhaba said, "Those two will be *Purohita* Mahapatra and Rajaguru Mahapatra. They will be at each fort where Gajapati would camp briefly and perform special rituals on their behalf. Be it for a day or two, the Lord Jagannath, in the defence, will be offered prayers. The *Purohita* Mahapatra's name is Sudarshan Rathasharma. He is one of the most renowned priests serving the deity at Jagannath temple. He has set a great example by performing established rituals in the temple and evening prayer, the aarati sincerely in his turn. He is also ready and interested to do the same now.

We must minutely obey when His Excellency commands. The construction of Jagannath temples, along with the performance of Puja and car festival in all castles of Odisha, has been nicely done as per schedule.

Rajaguru Mahapatra, always by your side, will be available to clear any of our doubts on religious matters. We should have a miniature Odisha with us. If there is any other command from your Excellency, *Antaranga* is ready to follow."

Gajapati said nothing. He only nodded in agreement. His face spoke amply about his full consent, filling *Antaranga* with immense joy. So no one else is to strain any more. All is well because Gajapati is happy.

But Gajapati's deep emotions were stalking his sense of mental satisfaction. He is pained for leaving his native land to its fate. He is withdrawing himself from the purview of Chakadola Jagannath, the Lord and the supreme power sustaining Odia's mindset. True, his relatives and family members have hurt him, and he thought their love for him would last for eternity. More unbearable is when anybody wounds his devotion to Jagannath, the passion that kept burning like an inextinguishable flame in the spiritual chamber of his mind. And that is visible on his face. In the last part of the eighth decade of his life, Gajapati alone knew how gloomy his future was. Since life usually is expected to be full of dreams, why should anyone think everything will end soon?

At this age, his errant mind has grown sensitive. Tears stream down his cheeks, and his voice chokes for every paltry matter. He is not able to hold them back. He is leaving Jagannath for his tour to the South. He is unable to give up his faith in Jagannath. He told himself that the two spiritual Mahapatras going with him would always remind him of Him.

"How can I give you up, O Lord? Why do I have fear in my heart, O Lord? There I see the distant South. Can my eyes return to see your charming face, O Lord, my pathfinder, my eternal guide?"

But then, *Antaranga* Uchhaba felt sympathetic for him. He thought, "Gajapati, the crest jewel of Odisha, is out to march on the unruly South in this age, the region he had earned by his genius.

However, his mind is full of fear, sadness and kind concern. Is there any chance for this great soul to be in danger far away from his native land? Why shan't I dissuade him from undertaking this hazardous task? Let him not go.

"No, it's just impossible. This man is Gajapati. He is not a man to relent. Still, I shall say a word and see." That filled him with a bit of courage.

Uchhaba opened his mouth," Your Excellency, I beg your pardon. It would be best if you were in Barabati now. I can go with the two Mahasenapatis to Kondavidu and join Parichhas Dakshina Kapileswar Mahapatra there, lead the soldiers and liberate the region on the banks of Cauvery from the enemy. The massive force of elephants and foot soldiers on our southern station is far more than those in the South. Of course, we can't ignore some forts like Bahamani, Vijayanagara and other small kingdoms."

Gajapati roared," How dare you *Antaranga* Mahapatra! Why do you think I'm a bugger? General Kapilendra, Gajapati Kapilendra Deva, has never been sluggish and silent. He is the man forever at the forefront of battles. How can he retreat in danger? Remember, age never makes a king imbecile in mind. You prepare the present army: I am ready to march to the South."

Antaranga's heart brimmed over with enthusiasm. Thanks, Lord, that he was heartily interested in campaigning to the South. He is second to none, and no one else can ever take his place.

Within a short time, Uchhaba was busy making arrangements for departure from Barabati Fort.

Barabati Forte

The Honeyed Touch of the Motherland

If we were to compile a list of Odisha's most patriotic sons based on their fervent ardour and intense zeal, Kharavela and Kapilendra Deva would undoubtedly emerge as worthy rivals for the highest accolade. However, it is this very Kapilendra Deva who finds himself reluctantly departing from beloved land of Odisha in the twilight of his life, driven by compelling circumstances.

The Gajapati's heart is heavy with the weight of departure; he is unwilling to bid farewell to his motherand. For him, life without the Barabati Palace and the presence of Lord Jagannath in Puri is inconceivable. Time, it seems, has dealt him a harsh hand, deeming him unworthy of continuing as the Emperor of Odisha. He is compelled to leave behind his motherland, his place of birth, and the rich tapestry of is culture, surrendering to the dictates of time. The path ahead appears uncertain, his mind is clouded, his hands tremble, and is face bears the burden of his internal turmoil.

To ensure a smooth departure, the Gajapati has issued strict orders that the queens are not to see him off. This directive is intended to prevent any potential disruption caused by emotional farewells and tearful outbursts from family members. Despite this, the Gajapati sits alone on his throne, lost in contemplation.

He grapples with conflicting emotions, caught in a dilemma imposed by the passage of time. Leaving his cherished Barabati Castle in Cuttack for the banks of the River Krishna in Vijaya Bahuda is a bitter pill to swallow. He envisions the distant riverbanks in his mind, but the prospect of returning to his palace in Cuttack feels uncertain and hazy. Emotions surge within him, and he harbours doubt about whether he will ever return alive. Everything that unfolds before him seems shrouded in uncertainty.

While fighting with the formidable armies of Vijayanagara or Bahamani, he must have rushed into the thick of the battle on horseback in the face of fear, anxiety and terror surrounding him then. Despite all that, the distance was not a deterrent for Kapilendra Deva. Gajapati's army sprang up in battle mode and marched into every corner of the kingdom with even the slightest trace of terror. Gajapati appeared there instantly from the faraway Barabati Castle of Bidanasi Cuttack. Soldiers drew strength from him and were battle-ready. War strategists all year round assessed the war potential of neighbouring affluent kingdoms. Odia army pounced upon the enemy in their time-tested ways at the behest of Gajapati. He and his intelligence network were the driving force of all these activities. He was interested in preparing this combat plan and was leading in attaching respectability and grandeur to the Odia army.

But why is it that today he is as apprehensive as ever before? He cannot understand why the present context is dragging him back from the southward march. Before this day, he could campaign southward irrespective of the geographical hurdles, not wasting even a moment, crossing rivers and creeks and hills and woods at the slightest hint of any danger to his kingdom from that direction.

Today, he has an unusual attraction for his motherland, which is standing in his way. He is at his wit's end as to why this native soil makes him so tender towards it. The tragic scene of his final departure plays out in his mind, with the recurrence of his entire life history providing the backdrop. The fragrance of native soil, air, water, and culture enchanted him momentarily. Is it a fact that he is leaving all this forever?

The play of the six seasons created an unprecedented vernal bloom in his mind, and they were all about the greetings of the mango season. The rain-soaked green forests were delighting his soul. The golden paddy fields in the season of dew were carrying a promise of plenty. God made the land green with corn and the greenery with his strength. Tears were welling up in his eyes.

"No, no, I can't forever desert my motherland." His soul writhed in anguish at the possibilities his doubtful mind wove. What a perception Lord Jagannath has given us to permeate the kingdom of Odisha with devotion! His playful ways have evolved many times, endearing them to one and all. The Lord is on a pleasure boat ride on a special occasion in Lake Narendra when devotees watch the holy scene in rapture. He is the ideal of every Odia. His miracles and playful ways socially have inspired me to live a joyful life independently. The Odia soul was cleansed spiritually into devotion to Lord's miracles. From time immemorial, that infinite power was procreating the sense of complete surrender to Him in His heart, which has generated it's defining speciality.

I don't feel like bidding farewell to my mother and transporting my body to the southern boundary. My heart and soul will stay back even if I do so. The Gajapati was terrified, and he trembled thinking about some unknown fear. It has been thirty long years since he held a holy broom to sweep on the car of Jagannath and sprinkle scented water. Not a year has passed when the Gajapati didn't do that service to the Lord at the Car Festival. How can he forget the sense of devotion for the deity that created immense earnestness and love for Him? The chime of gongs is shaping in his mind a sense of surrender to the eternal void, goading him to dedicate himself to that divine nothingness, capitulating to that omnipotent void to see this world bubbling with life. It has led to the rise of Odisha Rashtra and its destiny as the playfield of the Lord. Gajapati is His servant, His soldier, His "Rauta". How can the guard leave his master to travel far away from where death won't let him come back?

Sometimes after, he heard that his dear minister Gopinath Mahapatra wanted to meet him. *Antaranga* Uchhaba Bairiganjan soon welcomed him gracefully to the presence of Gajapati. Looking at his sad face, Gopinath Mahapatra said, "Your Majesty, today I see a strange thing. The man, who the world knows as tough enough not to shed tears, come what may, has a face flooded with it. Can tears drown the bloodshot fury in the eyes of a man who spent his whole life on the battlefield alone? He whose barest armour is the sword, whose heart flames with the fire of ferocity, tears in his eyes are not at all befitting."

Gajapati was silent. There was yet to be a reply from him.

Minister Gopinath began again, "In Jagannath temple of our Gopinathpur, people are praying for success in Your Majesty's southern campaign. You are marching far after a long period, and so all are worshipping the Lord for your good health and safe return."

Kapilendra Deva then began to speak, "All the duties of our generation are possibly over. I am in the

Gopinathpur Temple

thick of countless problems in power transfer. Lord Jagannath is the supreme commander of Odisha. Based on his divine portent, He selects the Gajapati of Odisha. But alas, this practice has ended in my family and the thoughts of our people."

"Strange is the process of choosing the heir in the royal family. So long as man harbours greed in his mind, the throne will surely fall in the hands of the greedy. It will destroy the time-tested practices and customs. Jagannath is the real custodian of Odisha Rashtra. Who can disregard His revelation in the dream?" Thus spoke on Minister Gopinath.

Gajapati rejoined, "Choosing the heir to a throne from among the royal family members is tricky. Last night alone, our spy stationed at Mewar passed us the latest news of the situation in Mewar Rajaputana. The fratricidal and patricidal incidents have occurred just for accession to the throne."

"I heard about Mewar and Chittor Forts. I know they swooped down on Muslim rulers; they could also crush Malwa Sultan," Gajapati changed the topic.

Minister Gopinath, his eyes dilated, dealt with the topic in detail, "Your Majesty knows history is strange. In this wide world, there is a second Kapilendra Deva even when the original Kapilendra Deva is very much there in Odisha!"

Everyone looked at the minister, awe-struck at the stunning news. Gopinath continued before Gajapati uttered even a word, "Gajapati ascended the throne at the beginning of *Kapilabda* (1434 AD). Rana Kumbha or Rana Kumbhakarna, in the same year, assumed control of Mewar. He fought against the alien rulers either in self-defence or by mounting attacks for spoils. He fell on Gujarat and Malwa and was successful too. And if we turn to Your Majesty, you battled with not two but many sultans who were your contemporaries, for instance, Ilias Sahi Sultan of Bangala, Sultans of Jaunpur, Bahamani and Malwa, that too, not in self-defence but in the direct military onslaught, thereby magnifying the image of Gangaraj Narasimha Deva. Narasimha Deva was more aggressive than defending Muslim rulers. You have attacked those Muslims exercising control over vast territories in such a manner that they will never think of invading Odisha so long as you are there in their memory.

"And Your Majesty, similarities with him don't end here. Rana Kumbha is your twin brother! He too is fond of dance and music, and his religious belief is for some deity - as Your Worship says you are a soldier of Jagannath, he also says he is the Dewan of Ekalingaji."

Gajapati felt relieved to know that there was another of his life in the person of Rana Kumbha. Rana also expressed his doubts about choosing his heir. Gajapati consoled himself with the thought that only Lord Narayana knows what is in store for Odisha, and it must be the best possible thing for us, he told himself. Now Gajapati and the Minister got into a confidential discussion. Then he seemed to be holding out hope because he kept listening attentively to the day-to-day affairs of the kingdom about his campaign southward.

Barabati Gate

Southbound Gajapati

The following morning was cold and foggy. The sun was hidden behind the mist and partially visible. But Gajapati's forces have begun moving southward at the first fall of light. After leaving Barabati, they would march on the road near Ekamra. Further South was the Kruttibash Mahadeva shrine, and still further was the sea and Lord Jagannath temple.

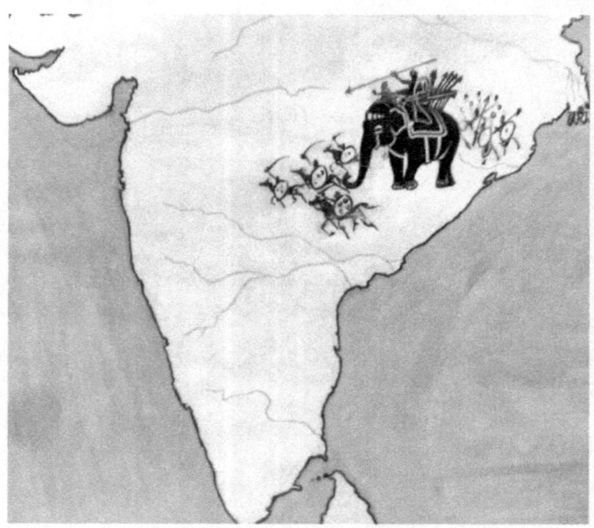

South Expedition of Odisha Elephantry

From there, they moved to the west and then again to the South. Gajapati saluted prayerfully Kruttibash Mahadeva from a distance. He is still preoccupied with the memory of the past decades back. It all happened in secret. There in the premises of Papanasini Temple near Kruttibash Mahadeva, Gopinath Mahapatra of Cuttack and Kasinath Mahapatra of Puri, accompanied by many other dignitaries and Ministers, became kingmakers after crowning Kapilendra as the King of Odisha. This secret never leaked out. They knew that Kapilendra, the General, could solve any upcoming problem as and when it arose. That secret happened. The last Ganga king failed in his mission to capture the southern side of Rajamahendry and couldn't return to the capital. Instead, he went into hiding at Gudari-Katak.

It all happened too soon. Thirty years ran away too soon to be known how. Yet when Ekamra knocked at the memory, that secret coronation prevailed in mind, and his heart brimming with joy. Antaranga was looking somewhere. Gajapati called him. "Had it been some other day, we would have travelled straight to south in the direction of Sri Kshetra."

Antaranga silently nodded his head. Lord Jagannath is only allowed to his devotee when He desires, rarely of the desire of the devotee," uttered slowly.

Gajapati bowed before Him with folded hands from a great distance. He was still determining if he would ever step on the sands of *Chakrateertha* at Purusottama Kshetra. The enchanting image of those spherical eyes of the Lord floated in front of his thought. But there was a difference: they were not looking at him with ever-open eyes as before; on the other hand, they were resting on him with infinite mercy and compassion.

Srimandira

Gajapati has acquired the status of being His greatest devotee only by his ardent reverence for Him. Like a few Ganga kings, he has shown himself as the soldier of "*Rauta*" and the greatest devotee of Jagannath. All the rituals meant for the Lord were the primary duty of the ruler. All His ordinations, His decree and dreams cannot be tampered with.

"Also the Sun Clock and the Konark Wheel comes to my mind," muttered Gajapati.

Gajapati's reflections on the downhill course of

his life reveal his deep sense of nostalgia and emotion. He acknowledges the relentless passage of time, using Sun Clock of Konark and ever-flowing tides of Mahodadhi as poignant metaphors. The memories of the Konark Sun Temple, a symbol of his grand legacy, occupy his thoughts. He yearns to witness the Konark wheel, a representation of his dreams and aspirations, one more time, but time itself remains an inexorable force, ceaselessly turning the wheel of life under the sun and moon. His contemplation leads him to a profound realisation that the Earth itself revolves, and any life that exists on it is inherently transient. This introspective moment highlights Gajapati's philosophical perspectives on the impermanence of existence before the eternal march of time.

The Konark Wheel

After a few hours, his couch passed through the twin hills of Kumarigiri and Kumaragiri. He recollected his old days of visit to the spot to see Ayur Maharaja almost half a century ago. Ayur Maharaja had set one target in his mind, and he was running after it all along. He saluted the great soul of Kalinga, who had created a political and cultural status which were unparallel in his times for his kingdom. He was satisfied that he could restore the glories of Odisha to the sublime extent. Tears of happiness rolled down his eyes.

Looking at the Lord's sympathetic eyes, tears rolled down his cheeks because he was asking himself why He was not smiling at him. His thoughts began to be confused like a skein of knotted yarn. When his horse-drawn coach started rolling up the rising slope of the hill at Khandagiri, his ideas could have been more straightforward. And in the meanwhile, he has been silently looking at the surrounding hills while crossing nearby the land of the native warriors of Odisha, the *Paikamala*.

Clusters of warrior settlements in the Khordha Pragana were the backbone of the invincible Gajapati army. He ordered the coachman to halt for a moment there. He stepped down and stood on the ground. He looked around and recognized that he had visited this place often with the *Paika Akhadas*. He intended to motivate the warrior race. This race is never scared to sacrifice its blood for the sake of its king and kingdom.

Odisha Paikas are much beyond any doubt for their bravery and dedication. They are staunch disciples of Lord Jagannath and accept life and death what Lord Jagannath has in store for them. They have vowed to protect Lord Jagannath from any intruder at any cost.

He picked up a fistful of soil and touched his forehead with it. He said, "This soil, the air and water on it, flora and fauna, have enriched the soul of Odisha." It struck him that all his innumerable conquests owed entirely to the land he stood on at that very moment. "I feel proud indeed. I am another resident of this land of warriors. In every battle, I can pull these people in large numbers to the battlefield. These are the men who carried and flaunted the flag of victory. Victory is the genuine warmth of their blood and the symbol of their war frenzy. They are fearless, sworn to the enchantment of *Mrutyu Sanjivani*. Does a soldier ever lose his life in battle? No. When he lays down his life in action, countless other young fighters rush from these hamlets. Life here is not a single water bubble, it is a concourse of thousands of bumps in the racing current of time, and this is the source of a thousand lives. The power of that current is real militarism. The Odisha Rashtra has evolved out of this *imperium in imperio*, the rule of the sword.

"The brave shall inherit the earth. *Paikamala*, the mother who has given birth to heroes, has nourished the Gajapati army well and has flown the victory banner with the support of all others. The name

"Paika" shivers down the enemy's spine. *Dhenkiya Dal,* warriors wielding swords and shields, or the attack groups of the *Aguani Thata,* the advance units or the first line to march and charge the enemy, could be as deadly as a leopard, or the *Dhanuki,* archers, could be unfailing when shooting at the target. In either case, they were invincible."

Gajapati, there, touched the earth and was transported with delight. His mind and soul were ecstatic. Peace and hope sprouted in his sad heart. He forgot his family feuds for a moment. The earth on which he stood has enabled him to hold in himself the endless supply of cosmic energy that powers life.

Aswarohi Paika

He went back to the coach and sat in it again. The caravan moved in the direction of Chilika past Barunei Mountain. *Antaranga* Mahapatra was close by. The horseman at the front was talking to the horses, now and then whispering in their ears, "Go slow and carry the King with perfect ease. Watch out for ups and downs on the path. Let not your discomforts in negotiating the rough road affect him." The King was not asleep but silent as if he was sleeping. It seemed he was thinking something new. These bumpy ways were not new to the King; they were all old.

south march

The *Pachhiani Thata*, the rear division guarding the flanks, was marching too. The elephant corps and the infantry followed at a distance, marching behind the Dagara. All received the information at the departure time from Barabati. *Antaranga* Mahapatra ordered the Gajapati's forces and guards to proceed to Kalingapatana. They needed no more information.

Five Mahapatras were riding near the King in tandem with the horse carriage. All of them were dressed in white apparel.

In Odisha, the minister was called Mahapatra. The

king's closest Mahapatra was *Antaranga* Mahapatra. Here that man was Uchhabaa Bairiganjan Mahapatra. The other five were *Sandhibigraha* Mahapatra, *Prasasanik* Purohita and *Rajaguru* Mahapatra. The kingdom of Odisha extended from Godavari in the South to far off north. Mighty and closely located military Forts governed the territory South of Godavari and Krishna. Parichchhas collected taxes. These taxes were deposited in the Odisha royal treasury as annual revenue. Gajapati conducted tours with many Mahapatras for these elongated kingdoms' governance, power transfer and public welfare.

On the way, *Antaranga* Mahapatra exchanged soothing words with Gajapati and whispered something in his ears. The Gajapati's sober face, at times, was shrouded in sorrow. Now and then, the swollen eyes shed drops of tears that dried up moments later. He looked ten years older within two days of the journey.

They reached the port settlements on the bank of Chilika after some time. Here is an old stable in Odisha. It was necessary to make arrangements for the tired elephant corps and cavalry on that long journey. Just then, *Antaranga* leaned suddenly towards Gajapati to attract his attention to his question.

He whispered," Your Highness, are the Forts in Karnat under our control in peril for some reason."

Gajapati said nothing. Bairiganjana could see that

Gajapati understood not a word of what he whispered. The feelings of depression were visible on his face.

After some time, Gajapati said clumsily, "The confidence and courage in me have fully collapsed. How can external forts arise if your inner forts have been smashed to smithereens?"

Antaranga replied gently, "Your Majesty, How can I explain to a great man like you? You take decisions independently according to your conscience. For today your decision is entirely personal. Let it be left to time to prove its long-term rightness. Please don't feel embarrassed. "

Gajapati shook his head in slight disagreement and said, "Can a man always be right? Could Ramachandra ascend the throne as per Dasaratha's desire?' Uchhabaa was listening to him attentively.

He replied, "When the Lord allows the devilry of wished Manthara, how can man's wish be fulfilled?"

It touched Gajapati's heart. He said, "True. Your suggestion is proper. There is undoubtedly some Manthara in my palace. Otherwise, why did she raise the issue of enthroning the youngest Purushottama, ignoring my eldest son, who was also the Crown Prince and heir apparent and my choice?

He thought Bairiganjan wanted to tell something but said nothing because such an unpleasant truth would hurt Gajapati.

Gajapati, on the other hand, urged him to go on, "Go on. We shall continue our progress on the way. What has happened at home, well, has happened. Now our immediate headache is Saluva Narasimha. For a year since, his violence has endangered our supremacy over Kondavidu, Udayagiri and Chandragiri in the South.

Antaranga Mahapatra saw that the team had passed Chilika. It was midday of the winter season. They couldn't go further. They must reach Chhatragarh limits before sundown. Otherwise, it would be a challenge to manage the tour of Gajapati.

Antaranga Mahapatra calmly told the coachman, "You must take us to the *Gajapati Nivas* at Chhatragarh before evening."

The coachman glanced at the west, marked the sun's position, started driving the coach faster, and said, "We shall be there in time. This carriage is closest to Gajapati's heart. It has made his presence felt in many a battle in adversity throughout his life. At times it has rushed from far away Kalabarga or Bahamani kingdom to Mandaran fort on the Bangla border to give its Nawab a fitting reply. The distance I can cover today is much less than those."

Antaranga was going to say something, but on Gajapati's face, he noticed a blank look. He turned to the coachman and said, "Gajapati is contemplating how best to remove the possibility of roadblocks in every work in days to come. For this reason, he kept a gigantic army ready, so he spent his life in military engagements. He has built his military forces under his direct supervision spanning many years. In this world, the knack for managing an enormous mastodon corps with foresight is known only to His Highness. That military competence was unimaginable till last year; today, for some internal reason, the new King, Saluva Narasimha, has dented it. Gajapati was busy with his family affairs for some days, so he could not analyze the seriousness of intelligence reports. And naturally, mice would be at play as the cat is out. "

The coachman heard all that but remained unimpressed. He responded with a casual surprise. He has got the privilege of being nearer to the Gajapati for long periods of his life. An amazingly mighty king who was with him for thirty-three years was a blessing to him. *Antaranga* Mahapatra had something to say, but his lips did not utter anything.

The sun was slipping down in the west. Chhatragarh was nearing. The river before Chhatragarh had become a slender stream. The coachman had the experience of taking this route through the river and had a sense of its depth. For the rainy season, a wooden bridge was there to pass on. The month of November, *Kartika* was over, and that of *Margasira* had begun. The water level had gone down, and it would not be a problem for the coach to cross it through. The coachman hoped they would soon reach Chhatragarh, just a stone's throw away. They arrived before nightfall. The fortress officials welcomed the King, who led him to his restroom.

All the Mahapatras arrived too. *Antaranga* Mahapatra explained their night stay arrangements, and after that, all of them met Gajapati. His Highness looked disturbed as before. His smiling face was lustreless and lacked brilliance and vitality.

A messenger from the north arrived at that time. He hesitated to share the news about Mandaran Fort. Antaranga understood the reason and clarified, "Here, six Mahapatras, all confidants of Gajapati, are present. Deliver the news at once."

The messenger then said, "I am Dharani Uttarakabata. His Majesty had administered oath to me for this spy work. I shall work in the nation's interest and remain faithful to him. I felt he is in the dark about what is happening in Mandaran Fort. Our soldiers there are far more potent than those of Bangla Sultan Ruknuddin Barabak. Despite this, we had to retreat. The reasons are coming out piecemeal.

"The present army general of the forces deployed on the northern limits has become a good friend of our enemy Rukuddin's army general. They may have worked out some secret *quid pro quo*. Our army retreated from a part of the Gauda kingdom in our control for the last twenty years. Many greedy and traitorous people on our side have done this heinous work."

Gajapati started to agitate in a fury at these words and said, "I had dreamt of forming a highly qualitative military force. My priority was to gain their loyalty through faith. And it had given dividends; today, Odisha's prosperity and power are prominent in Bharatavarsha. As I was busy with my internal family quarrels and was away from administrative affairs, the *Uttarakabata*, guardian of the military fort, gave way to the enemy. Muslim forces captured the Mandaran Fort. So long as Mandaran was ours, it could keep the Muslims away. The border force at this place for the last twenty years didn't allow them to invade Odisha, not to speak of plundering our treasury. The fear of Muslim invasions had disappeared. Presenting Jagannath in his golden attire in public was the proof of the absence of that fear."

This secret message fell on Gajapati's keen ears. At one time, what to speak of Ruknuddin Barabak, Delhi Badshah forces also had come to penetrate the northern border. Odisha could fight for ten to fifteen days. Strangely, the highly skilled Odisha army retreated without resistance even though Barabak did nothing. Gajapati could never expect this. When you look the other way, false friends will infest everywhere. My own General has turned traitor. Hence always, caution is necessary under all circumstances.

Purohita Mahapatra arrived after arranging the sacramental fire in the Jagannath temple adjacent to

Chhatragarh and prayed to Gajapati to proceed to the temple.

Gajapati's fury hadn't subsided. However, he forgot all his sorrow in the name of Jagannath. He purified his soul with these four letters. His butter-soft soul mellowed and melted further as he thought Jagannath had given him everything he has today. He bowed before Him and put all his intense agony at His disposal. The moment he uttered His name, the flame of his piety shot up in its entire splendour.

After a long gap, Gajapati spent a night in Chhatragarh Fort. It is many years since he put his foot in this tiny fort. All his life has been on battlefields. His grandfather was a General in the Odishan army. His father, too, had vowed to protect the life of Odias. He was appointed General at a comparatively young age due to his extraordinary military acumen. He could establish himself as a distinguished horse rider and warrior because of his sense of confidence. His handsome figure and gentle behaviour took him to the proximity of Gangaraj Bhanudev fourth.

It's undoubtedly Jagannath's blessing to have personal acquaintance with Gangaraj. This familiarity honoured him as one of his most credible relatives. He was hence appointed a security officer. Simultaneously, he performed duties in the palace and with the military forces. The King asked him to perform even the responsibilities of a mediator when he needed secret diplomatic understanding or military counsel from the neighbouring kings.

Gradually it became his daily work to perform duties as the head of military and diplomatic affairs. A famous and proactive ruler can perform all these duties efficiently, but it would not be accessible if the King took no interest in administrative matters. Kapilendra had many times been insulted for this reason in the court of neighbouring kingdoms. The silence and soft words of Gangaraj had exposed his weakness before them. Kapilendra had witnessed such royal indifference for the past ten years at Bidanasi Cuttack.

Gajapati slipped into deep thought. He recalled how he had built his army on the strength of his faith. Similarly, the Paika army accepted his authority based on faith. He had inspired such loyalty; they never hesitated to shed their blood for freedom and conquests. Taking advantage of his involvement in family feuds, how could Uttarakabat's treachery go against his interest? In such a scenario, how come Ruknuddin or Gauda King be wrong? I have chosen traitors masquerading in trustee's cloak.

He had to accept that it was his incapability. There was a time when Utkal broke into pieces, and Kapil Rautray united it to rebuild a powerful Odisha. Today he is endowed with the additional power of Gajapati title, and if at such a time the kingdom loses its territory due to betrayal, it's pure mismanagement.

What else could it be? Of course, his last days were far from peaceful; he was very anxious and gloomy. He needs help to ascertain if his decision was right or wrong. The Lord will take all the decisions. He has always been working to perform the Lord's decree and works with great respect for His will.

Gajapati was in deep contemplation. He was telling himself, "I have not seen the dream. Pārvati could not have told me a lie, and that, too, in the name of Jagannath. Not once but many times, Jagannath alerted her in dreams, alerting her endlessly that Purushottama alone was worthy of the throne. Most likely, He ordained through someone else; I shall follow that path only. We must carry out his orders. But everyone else is opposed to the idea. And it's not just a few days that this has happened; it's for the last ten years that the restlessness has been brewing. To escape from family feuds and work for army unity has become difficult."

"Well, we must follow the command of the Lord. Where does the question of my success or failure arise in such a case? I have always been looking for His revelation in my dreams like a thirsty swallow looking up for rain. He will direct me. Had He wished I should crown my eldest son Hamvira Deva my chief queen or I would have seen the dream. How come it was Pārvati Devi who got the decree in her dream? Let the whole world collapse, let the kingdom go to hell, let all the conscientious persons oppose me. Jagannath and

His ordinations are supreme for me. On the strength of this unwavering faith in Him, only the Kapila of yesterday has become the Lord's soldier. Whatever I have done is by me but by the grace of Lord Jagannath. During these thirty-three years, he had built Odisha into a new form with his full strength and wisdom. But in reality, the supreme Lord has done all that."

The messenger present there expected Gajapati would roar in anger. He wondered what Gajapati was saying. Gajapati is excusing all the wrongs in the name of Jagannath. He expressed no interest in recapturing the north boundary. Mahapatras were also stunned to hear his opinion. Each one of them was like his own kith and kin. They knew his mind. That's why they wondered how Gajapati, short-tempered, accepted failures in the name of the Lord.

Gajapati Kapilendra Deva is a robust figure with a smiling face. But this amiability doesn't mean too much behavioural resilience, the kind of elasticity in hibiscus cannabis, the stem of a jute plant with shorn of fibres. He would instead break but not bend. Today the world finds his strange manners. He considered Mandaran to be Odisha's vulnerable northern pass. So he posted formidable guards there and, after that, got engaged in the conquest of the South for two decades.

Today is the first time he gets a hint of betrayal in his army. Gajapati has not taken it seriously. It is outside Gajapati's rule book. Instead, it can be considered a change in Kapilendra's character. It's all game time playing with us. Gajapati finds a split in his army into opposite factions.

Again *Purohita* Mahapatra indicated Antaranga Mahapatra to intrude and request the King that the evening sacramental fire rituals in Jagannath temple are on and all eagerly await His Majesty's presence.

Gajapati attended the rituals. He got engaged in discussions with all his Mahapatras. Rajaguru Mahapatra began calculating how soon they would reach the southern boundary. They will keep moving along the way with an eye on comfort by resting suitably to overcome travel-generated physical stress. Marching fast would drain their energy. They will fall sick. Gajapati had often gone by the traditional Cuttack-Rajamahendry road, but today, his age has stood as his barrier. Those days of fierce fighting on horseback are no more there.

Gajapati protested, "We must reach the southern border as soon as possible. Please don't reduce the speed for my comfort. This body has turned into a rock in my past life of frequent battles. The enemy's plans will burst like bubbles if we reach the soonest. "

All the Mahapatras, including *Antaranga* Mahapatra, requested Gajapati: marching so far with too much physical fatigue would bring misery upon us, they urged him. The body can't sustain pain under the pressure of old age; hence it would be proper to balance our speed with the ability to move without physical indisposition.

Gajapati replied, "You have all known and seen the fruit of lightning action. It so happened at Devarakonda of Telangana. Eight years ago, Bahamani Sultan Humayun Khan dispatched forces to kill Devarakonda chief Vellama Madiya Linga. Before they surrounded him from all sides, on Vellama's request for refuge, the Gajapati swift and violent military appeared there in no time. Our blitzkrieg worked out so well that Bahamani hung his head in shame. In their wildest imagination, they never thought the Gajapati army would reach Linga so fast."

What Mahapatras learnt from this military experience made them never put any proposal before Gajapati if it differed from his ideas.

They decided to start early the following day for Kalingapatana and then retired to rest.

Kalingapatana

As Gajapati Kapilendra Deva and his forces made their way to Kalingapatana, the weight of his responsibilities and the challenges of maintaining his vast empire weighed heavily on his shoulders. His concerns about the potential threats to his territory, particularly from Saluva Narasimha's advances added to his anxiety.

Kapilendra Deva's determination and resilience were evident in his ability to keep moving forward despite his old age. He remained vigilant, fully aware that the stability of his reign depended on his ability to defend his empire from external threats and internal challenges.

The dynamic between these historical figures and the ever-changing landscape of their time make for a compelling backdrop for the novel's narrative. Kapilendra Deva's struggle to maintain his rule and protect his kingdom adds depth and intrigue to the story.

For this reason, Gajapati was restless. Once he reaches there, he will rejuvenate his soldiers. Again, they will muster courage and be ready to defend their land. He expected a lot of things like this.

Gajapati called for *Antaranga* Mahapatra and ordered, "It would be helpful if we reached Kalingapatana early. We shall rest there for one and a half days and then continue. The scene is changing fast. We must hasten to the forts today itself before the enemy attacks them. Whenever my army is out of my sight, its strength is dwindling. Is it that the forces away from their native land are feeling restive? This thought of mine must be wrong because these people of Odisha have travelled to distant places in sail-driven ships. Distance, therefore, is acceptable for Odia people. But Gajapati's proximity bolstered their spirit and boosted their mental strength.

The coachman has explained to *Antaranga* Mahapatra that the coach can't take them to Kalingapatana. It's at least a hundred miles, and they have to cross two rivers on the way. It will be two days before they reach there. They must sojourn for a night at Ichhapura or some other military campsite.

Antaranga Bairiganjana spoke to him in a low tone; Gajapati has taken this route how many times no one knows. The whole army knows about this urgent and sudden army movement. By all means, we shall reach the nearest resting place before evening sets in. You drive the coach as fast as possible.

As desired, Gajapati arrived at Kalingapatana Fort before time. The Ganga dynasty founded the Fort much before. When the ancestors of Chodaganga Deva made Mukhalingam City their capital on the northern Bank of Vansadhara River, Kalingapatana, at the mouth of river Vansadhara, was famous for naval trade in past centuries. It owed its busy life to commercial and business activities of Kalinga from time immemorial with reputed East Asia region as well as Java, Sumatra and other groups of islands to the east of Bharatavarsha, popularly known as *Suvarna Dwipa*, the Golden Islands. Like all the harbours on the shore of Kalingasagar, its extent of business kept the settlements quite bustling with activities.

That small colony on the bank of Vansadhara became a strategic fort due to frequent campaigns by Narasimha Deva to the South. Suitable resident military bases confer power. It created a small Kalinga military base consisting of some soldiers and other military personnel, cavalrymen and war elephants. It was a temporary resting place for Gajapati and his feudal chiefs whenever they campaigned south. Rest houses for Gajapati and other officers and an office for other subordinate staff were ready. There is a Jagannath temple at Kalingapatana Fort in the tradition of Odisha. Kalingapatana on Kalingasagar has a colossal stronghold, the one to strengthen the South.

Gajapati's forces arrived at Kalingapatana. The Guards deployed there welcomed them with due honour.

Gajapati ordered, "Inform the Mahapatras to complete their morning work and to assemble in the meeting hall. All of them will join the rituals in Jagannath temple after the meeting."

Kalingapatana meeting hall carried a lot of importance. Southern division offices met there. Kalingapatana formed the highway for the Gajapati troop movement. It is the marching route and points at the direction contingents of infantry, cavalry and elephant forces would take.

Everything happened as per the order. The meeting began as soon as all officials assembled. Gajapati said, "Today, we have come to a place to fulfil our desires. I got this experience in my life. I halted here, and I completed my work without any glitches. In my first expedition, I stayed at Chhatragarh Fort and took eight years to subjugate Khemundi Gangas. They were Gangaraj Bhanudev's kin. When I entrusted the duty to wrest the administration of Odisha from the enemy's control, *Matta* Bhanudev, for months, enjoyed the hospitality at his friend's house. Still, I was busy with the recapture of Rajamahendry from the Reddy administrator on the southern border of Odisha. As a result of Bhanudev's apathetic military inertia, Reddy rulers were able every year to take villages administered by Odisha into their control, and the boundary of Odisha rapidly shrank. Jaunpur Nawab and Banga Nawab Nasiruddin felt that anarchy in Odisha was a fact, so there was a forewarning they would capture Odisha.

All the ministers and officials were restless. Their attempts to bring Gangaraj back were futile. What more could he do as a mere General except defend the kingdom and its temples? By this time, many feudal chiefs of Odisha had become opposed to Odisha Gajapati.

Gangaraj *Matta* Bhanudev, too, had no relationship with the feudatories. Where is the time for him? He drowned himself in intoxicants, and all the ministers could not but know that. Besides, he is too much effeminate. All day, he was spent with alcohol or queens in the harem. This news spilt out of the palace into the public domain. The word *"Matta"* was attached to his name.

Who can say what calamity would fall on Odisha in such circumstances? There is a rumour that Odisha would merge into Nasiruddin's Bangala. Here in Puri, the disciples of the Lord were apprehensive with panic. Jagannath temple servitors have become worried for fear that Nasiruddin and his army will plunder the temple treasury. The Odisha army resisted for ages. The Muslim marauders succumbed to their swords, and forced religious conversion may ensue in this virgin soil.

Is it a fact that Bhanudev is at war with Rajama-hendry Reddy? Or is he hiding in Odadi Chalukya's palace and enjoying life? He has not also asked for any message to send a military force from Odisha. In such a scenario, what kind of battle is Gangaraj fighting? Soldiers, temple inmates and people of Odisha talked many things about it. As at Puri, Jagannath servitors are exceedingly terrified, and employees at Bidanasi Cuttack are uniting to hit on some alternative. Gopi-nath Mahapatra and his group are foremost among Cuttack residents. Gopinath himself is an army Com-mander. He has full knowledge of Jaunpur. That pow-erful group of soldiers has started saying that *Matta* Bhanudev is hiding for fear of the enemy. If there is no immediate successor to the throne of Odisha, it will cease to be an independent kingdom.

"One day at midnight, it so happened that an elit-ist crowd led by Gopinath Mahapatra came to Barabati military camp to explain and said in a chorus, "We will crown you as the King of Odisha. *Matta* Bhanudev has gone for hiding somewhere. He is a gone case. We de-mand firm defence of our motherland. We must take action in time; otherwise, we will lose everything."

"I was shocked at this demand. I am a prominent supporter of *Matta* Bhanudev, a central source of his stability. I can't betray him. I assured them that I would manage the borders of Odisha till his return from the South. They consulted among themselves for a while and then said in one voice, 'No, that's your allegiance to him. He has no right to sit on the throne, even for a day. Here, the kingdom is in danger; he remained absent in the capital for six months to recover territory lost many years ago. By this behaviour, he has not only shown his irresponsibility but has also given an open invitation to the enemy to invade Odisha. "

And they also decided, "This Wednesday, the second day of the bright fortnight in the month of Shravan, August 1434 A.D., in the afternoon at Ekamra Kshetra, Bhubaneswar, in Papanasini Temple near Kruttibash, the crowning of Kapilendra Deva will take place, and the fact of the matter will subsequently be engraved on the temple wall of Kruttibash."

Coronation

Gajapati went on, "I had no words. Only there was one request: first, let my master Emperor Bhanudev return; we will conduct all these functions in his presence. He will certainly wholeheartedly support this proposal. When childless Gangaraj has accepted me as his foster child, it is proper on his part to accept this proposal of mine. "

Some in the crowd reasoned, "Why won't he accept our proposal? He will appear if Odisha hasn't surrendered to Muslim control. And most likely, Odisha must have been lost to Muslims by now. Such an effeminate and hopeless ruler cannot but accept our proposal. Besides, he is present in the capital with no qualms. Muslim footmen are keeping account of all this. No doubt, they are also all ears to our decision. "

I expressed my inability and said firmly, "I won't ascend the throne till Gangaraj returns." But they were ready to crown anyone except Bhanudev in the kingdom's interest. The Odisha army was considering an alternative in secret, not simply ministers and other officials. All the army men under my generals heartily wanted me to ascend the throne. One of the soldiers shouted, "In Odisha, every moment has turned hazardous. At the time of war, the kingdom and Jagannath are naturally in peril. Whatever Bhanudev has done in his reign, he has only fed the enemy's hunger for Odisha.

Even if powerful kings like Narasimha Deva stayed at Bidanasi Katak, strong border security forces always guarded the border. But Bhanudev, lost in utter sensual pleasures day in and night, has been indifferent to the day-to-day affairs of the kingdom. He never took an interest in the art of day-out fighting and needed help leading an army. Apart from this, he rarely encouraged his army to guard Odisha's boundaries."

"Gopinath Mahapatra was not a man to give up so easily. He silenced me with his patriotic words. I just looked at them silently to see how they would transfer power.

Gopinath Mahapatra indeed proved so much more capable in my reign! He was a mighty Mahapatra in Ganga rule. He had assured me of fearless protection, "Let the king of Odisha invest in me the responsibility of the northern border, and then rest assured there would be no enemy infiltration from that side."

"I also forgot fully the northern limits in my lifetime. It wasn't wise to turn my eyes from the South to the North and the annexation of Banga. He was the greatest well-wisher I knew. His father, Laxman Mahapatra, was the royal priest, and his elder brother was Minister Aditya Narayana Mahapatra. On this day, he came from Gopinathpur village near Paga, some fourteen miles from the Fort at Barabati. His family built a Jagannath temple there and inscribed 60 lines of Odia script on stone about Gajapati's rule. He was a conservative Brahmin. Warm blood coursed through his veins. He was second to none so far as national interest was concerned. So, the enemy by no means could penetrate the northern military base.

Indeed, when this vast empire of Odisha is

swallowed in time's dreadful jaws and faded from public memory, Gopinath temple will be the mute witness to our superb affluence and enrich the pages of history.

Odisha of such enormous size built up till *Kapilabda* 20, 1464 AD in the Gregorian calendar, perhaps never was seen in the past. No one can conceive the future, but one could never think of an Odisha so large. A lot can be known about this only from stone inscriptions."

Gajapati paused after saying all those words at a stretch. For a moment, the strain of sorrow waned from his face. Past glory, to some extent, alleviated his present mental agony.

Construction of the Kalingapatana Jagannath temple enhanced the strength of the southern command of Odisha. Kalingapatana is the identification mark of Odia pride in the South during the reign of Chodaganga and Narasimha Deva. However, Gajapati Kapilendra Deva is wide awake, for before his eyes, his hard-earned empire of Odisha is shrinking, and such information is frequently coming to his knowledge. The danger is stalking him from all directions at the same time. He had prostrated before Lord Trinity. Perhaps he dozed off on the temple floor. The night was getting deeper.

Neither *Antaranga* Bairiganjana nor *Purohita* Mahapatra dared to break his meditation. Gajapati needs to gain a sense of time and space. Many incidents are dancing before his eyes closed in half-sleep.

Hamvira Deva is asking for an explanation, "Why did you wrest the throne from me?"

Kapilendra Deva's heart shivered. His lips fumbled. Hamvira Deva again roared, "Why did you showcase me as the heir-apparent and for twenty years engage me in royal assignments? What immoral deed I did for which you took such a cruel and heartless decision?"

No answer emerged from Kapilendra Deva's soul. But there was Jagannath before both the son and the father. There was a charming smile on his face as ever.

Hamvira Deva didn't pause; he continued, "If such deceitful thought sat in your mind, how could you relish my success in performing the gravest duties of the kingdom and then conspire in yourself to disappoint me? Lord Jagannath didn't reveal so in your dreams. You are discriminating at the instigation of someone else. Despite being Lord Jagannath's greatest devotee, how could you make such an unkind decision? Have you forgotten Bhakta Prahallad, too, got justice from Him?

Dasaratha is asking Ramachandra to go into exile in the forest. Father seeking son's expulsion is a rarely-seen negative twist in our mythology. The same kind of deadly time has come to Odisha today. The shadow of Dasaratha falling on Gajapati's head is tearing the whole monarchy into shreds. My father has never in his life committed an iota of wrong. Indeed, this thought whirled his mind with the story of Manthara of Ramayana. He is treating his heir apparent to the throne as if he is a disinherited one. How can peace come to him in the last days of his life?"

The king is highly distressed at such a dream seen in light sleep. Then, deep sorrow swallowed him up. For a moment, he fell fast asleep. There was a violent storm in his mind. He saw all the officials posted in the South staring at him together. Each one of them looked like one Hamvira Deva. They were glaring at him with eyes wide open. And with them, he saw the Bahamani emperor! Bahamani king shouted, "Hey Kapilendra Deva Gajapati, how long will you rule over such a large kingdom? Give us Rajamahendry and Simadri."

Gajapati was stimulated to wakefulness. He screamed, "No, no, not at all possible. Gajapati of Odisha is not so weak. Aren't you the same Bahamani emperor whose forces were smashed once by only ten thousand soldiers under my command, and you accepted defeat simply at the sight of my elephant corps? How much vigour do you have that you brag and bluster vainly? So long as Kapilendra Deva is alive, can anyone take not an inch of land from the captured territory? Bahamani Muslim kingdom has the trait of being rude. Gajapati has already tested his strength. Why should he care for his vain bragging?"

When Gajapati was in a prone position before the duty, all the officials were waiting restlessly for him; the moment Gajapati was his usual self, he went to his palace. Gajapati was urged to inspect the soldiers' morning drill the following day. Odisha drew its strength only from wrestling, exercising and soldiers' training and swordsmanship. And for this, the *akhadas* or gymnasiums have been built all over the kingdom. But each Fort of Odisha had a general and, for emergencies, thousand-foot soldiers, elephant riders and cavalrymen.

Kalingapatana is now a larger township and a substantial military base. Forces to the countless strongholds of the south fan out from this Fort. Kapilendra Deva himself has inspired Kalingapatana resident forces into Odia militarism.

Gajapati put a question to the thousands of soldiers out to honour the emperor, "Many from amongst you have returned from the southern strongholds. How does the general public view Odia administrators and Odisha governance?"

Some cavalrymen had spent much time with the ordinary folks, so they vividly narrated their impressions. The gist of their comments was that the people in the South were fond of Gajapati rule. For religious reasons, they are not interested in being under Muslim control. Personal freedom was curtailed to the least by Gajapati. Besides this, he is known as the servant of Lord Jagannath and hence commands infinite respect and loyalty from the Hindus as king of Puri; they, too, bend before him, treating him as the living image of Jagannath."

"Bravo, ye Odia warriors. I express my deep satisfaction with the input about the public you have gathered from the general public. The Gajapati army is not limited to the conquest of territory alone; our primary goal has been to protect the people from Muslim oppression. Muslims are involved in many despicable activities. There are instances of them selling our people abroad as enslaved people. Can Gajapati tolerate this? Putting a stop to their cries of distress has also been one of the goals of our campaigns. We have punished Bahamani for the misdeeds of his general, Sanjir Khan, who was doing horrible things and engaging in the slave trade. We have inflicted punishment on him to such an extent that he had to stop such activities as long as the Gajapati army was in battle mode. He will never have the guts to challenge Odisha. The public must have got the smell of this. They must have followed our steps as an example of humanism. This religious and devotional reason is most important. They have no other alternative than to love and support Odisha.

Odia race has shown virtue in the captured kingdoms. The Lord himself is with this race. Bells ring in all its temples. The temple premises look clean, and the temple shines. The deities of each temple are there beside Jagannath. And the people's dream of travelling to Purushottama Kshetra, the Puri, grows towards a viable possibility.

Three days have passed by now. Looking at the alertness and zeal of the resident forces there,

Gajapati returned his lost peace to some extent. He was encouraged to find that Odia Paika has kept sight of his goal, even on bad days. Again, Gajapati's manliness sprang up in him. His war hunger was not gone even at the age of eighty. For half a century, the Paika army he had built utilizing Odisha's human, livestock, and material resources has taken this unique form in contemporary Bharatavarsha.

One of the most vigorous patrons of Odisha's Gajapati army is Kapilendra Deva. Joining the military in his youth, he weighed up its strength or ideally managed its human resources and conducted threadbare research on how varieties of Odisha resource materials could be utilized in warfare to ensure victory. Retired army men of the kingdom established an institute for war training. Otherwise, how could the sturdy fighters from the grassroots level of Odisha get trained to strengthen them to bring up the rear guard for the Paika army? How could ordnance factories of Odisha produce weapons aplenty and despatch them to training centres and battlefields? In addition to this, discovering new horizons in military strategies was Kapilendra Deva's speciality. Techniques of offence and defence in war admit of myriad varieties. The valorous war preparedness of the Gajapati army strangely reduced the spontaneous invasion from territories.

Training centres for strategic planning were estimating enemy strength through intelligence reports.

He incorporated these inputs in military planning to enable Odia Paikas to respond appropriately to enemy onslaughts at the right time.

Gajapati Kapilendra Deva, from his lifelong experience, has been convinced that for war and warrior, time and opportunity must be favourable to ensure victory. Therefore, waiting for the fortunate circumstances was vital. Striking the enemy at the right moment lays the march to victory.

Gajapati had an irresistible desire to visit Kalingapatana harbour. He felt that not seeing it would make him deeply regretful late in life. He ordered the Fort to arrange his trip to Kalingapatana with his entourage to satisfy himself.

A horse-drawn coach could be ready without delay, and all the Mahapatras followed him on horseback. They entered the principal office of the harbour. Birupakshya Gajendra, the head of the port, was present there.

There was a time when this harbour was operative for the naval forces of Kalinga. All those harbours mentioned in history, like Dantapur, Mukhalingam, Kalinganagar, Bishakhapatana, Machhalipatnam and Pithunda, continued as such because of their depth and strategic locations. However, innumerable harbours had come up on the coast of Kalinga and disappeared with time. The rivers carried alluvial soil to the basin, which raised the seabed. As a result, ships stopped coming to take on or discharge cargo. The result harbours stopped running. Popularly, it is a fact that the people of Kalinga were brave. They used to begin their sea journey right from home, located near the sea. Harbours were close to each other. Thus, ports had been changing from locality to locality, and the maritime trade was the natural profession of the then Odia race.

After Gajapati entered Kalingapatana port city, his love for the sea swelled. He sent for Antaranga Mahapatra and asked, "Hello, Mohapatra, how is our overseas trade?"

Antaranga Mahapatra replied, "Your Majesty, you have been putting this question to this servant of yours many times, and I have been giving my replies, but you forget them promptly. When there was an expectation at Purushottama Kshetra that Kapilendra Deva would construct a mammoth temple, you quoted the canon of Odisha kings. You said, "The foundation stones of Ekamra, Puri and Konark temples were constructed with donations by my forefathers from their earnings in overseas trade. Feudatories provided tools and a labour force for the construction. All the competent artisans and sculptors together ventured to join the spectacular work. In this way, we have constructed our Kruttibash temple and row of temples at Bhubaneswar, Puri Jagannath Temple and Konark Sun Temple. It was difficult for me to build temples because I had spent all my time defending our territorial limits."

"Your Majesty has spent much time on campaigns outside the kingdom as on military preparation and planning. You had spared no time even for your family. Where do you have a scope to pay attention to Odisha's almost ruined sea trade? Of course, for the last couple of centuries, merchants, not of Odisha alone but of the kingdoms flanking the whole sea on the east, have been withdrawing themselves from mercantile trade because deep into the sea, pirates have endangered their lives and property.

Although several decisions were taken before in the reign of Narasimha Deva regarding this, even his attempts failed to protect the sea from pirates' hold. The oldest merchants have wound up their business. Only occasionally, passenger ships are voyaging to Java, Sumatra or Bali. Piracy has become an occupation in the sea and a hazard for Odisha Sadhabas. Undoubtedly, Arabian pirates will destroy sea trade not only of Odisha alone but also of the Eastern seaboard.

Antaranga Mahapatra glanced at Gajapati to read the effects of his statement and waited silently for his response.

Gajapati's face became red in anger and distress.

Gajapati shouted, "Leave it, Mahapatra. Let that matter rest awhile. Let's keep our heads over that where there is no chance of any substantial action. I have thought over this issue many times. Our culture minister has furnished me with all the related details.

Along with Narasimha Deva, many Ganga kings were interested in the merchants' well-being. They collectively sent messages to the rulers of Java, Bali and Tamrapalli (Sri Lanka). He took steps to the best of his ability but in vain. It was as accessible for the pirates to hide in the vast expanse of the sea as it was difficult for us to give protection to the merchants' ships.

"It's true. You can understand that when these Arabians set out with their mariner's compass for commerce with eastern kingdoms, our naval trade had peaked by then. They didn't confine themselves to competition in business only; they involved their country's slave traders and captured our merchants and crew to sell in other countries. A rumour has spread in Telangana that some top military officers of the Bahamani kingdom are involved in such horrendous activities. Bahamani kingdom is, for this reason, at war. We are fighting on the side of the people. On the land route, one high official named Sanjar Khan sent the civilian population to slave markets in foreign lands. They are involved in slave trafficking. Vile and detestable are those impious, wicked creatures.

"Mercantile trade was the ancestral occupation of Kalinga-Utkal. Now that the billowing tide has turned into a timid ebb, our Odia people have, in large numbers, settled in the whole of Suvarna Island thousands of years before Bardhaman Mahavira and Buddha appeared on the earth. Many successors of the Kalinga dynasty had been rulers in these islands. Jagannath temple, Buddhist monasteries and monuments are there in Odisha. Our sculptors also live there, and our architecture has spread to those islands. Those Odia colonies, so to speak, got separated from the original kingdom of Odisha with the Arabian's entry with piracy.

Today, we are neck-deep in trouble. It is no longer possible to communicate with them. These Afghan Turkish Arab people have been hitting hard at our culture. Although they found sea routes to our land, they have ruined our culture by preaching religiosity devoid of humanism, dirty deeds like piracy and the slave trade."

There was nothing more to discuss on naval trade. Still, all the Mahapatras dispersed for the night because the following day, they would march to Simadri at dawn, leaving Kalingapatana behind.

Gajapati Image

Fort Simadri of Bell-Bronze Doors

Gajapati Kapilendra Deva's decision to resume the march southward without dalay, driven by a dream he had the previous night, left his followers bewildered and concerned. Thay could only speculate about the reasons behind this abrupt decision. The dream seemed to have deeply affected him, and it was clear that he was grapping with various worries and uncertainties. One of the primary concerns was the potential threat from Vijayanagara, which had been expanding and posed a significant challenge to Gajapati's rule. The recent developments in Mandaran and the possibility of Kondavidu slipping out of control added to his anxieties. Furthermore, Gajapati's suspicion extended to his own family, particularly his elder son, who was currently estranged from him and gathering forces in the South. The fear of potential alliances or betrayals within his family weighed heavily on Gajapati's mind, leaving him in a state of confusion and doubt.

The dream seemed to have shaken Gajapati's

confidence and forced him to take swift and decisive action, even if the reason behind his action were not entirely clear to his followers.

Even at eighty, the thirst for a war of Gajapati Kapilendra Deva did not quench. His warmongering has been gone for fifty years of fighting on the battlefield. He wants to maintain every inch of land he has ruled over in his lifetime. Now, he hastens towards the South, apprehending Vijayanagara's assault.

Fort Simadri was a two-day march from Kalingapatana. They can reach there before sunset if they start early in the morning. Every month, the Paika army kept moving to and fro between these two forts. On the way to the South from Odisha, they always pass by Simadri. And it's the southern administrative headquarters. It is very high on the Eastern Ghats, far from the sea.

Gajapati alone is on the move in a horse-drawn coach towards Simadri. Like the Aguani Thata, the advanced units of first in line to march or charge in battle formations, one military team composed of sturdy cavalry units and double their number of horse rider archers were running ahead of him. Each time Kapilendra marches on this inaccessible route when he enters the dense jungle of Eastern Ghats from the coastal plains, his confidence in his strength multiplies, and his heart swells with pride. There was a day when he ascended the throne as Gajapati. This Simadri, under the Reddy's control, stood in his way.

Indeed, Simadri was a military and administrative centre in southern Odisha during the Ganga rule. The Utkal king had an administrator posted as the feudal chief of both Odadi and its adjacent lands. Since they are far-off regions from Cuttack and Kalinga, kings tried to annex Odadi and Telangana. It is also a fact that the people of this region, Hindus as they were, wanted to be at a safe distance from the greatly enhanced Yavan military surrounding them and so wanted to live under the protective hand of Odisha.

Wise and experienced Kapilendra smiles when Odadi comes to his mind. He thought this time, and when they reached Simadri, he would unfold the events of twenty years ago to the assembly of Mahapatras. After leaving Kalingapatana, they were on the second day of their journey.

It was almost evening. Simadri was farther away. But must reach their destination. It is the dense jungle of the Eastern Ghats. Despite massive armies of cavalry and archers, the night always belongs to wild animals. Of course, the Administrator of Simadri Fort had dispatched a two-hundred-strong Paika army unit, which had arrived at the halfway point. Even if it was just evening, the danger was on the way. No specific fear might affect Gajapati, but his forces were apprehensive that dejected Prince Hamvira Kumar was touring the South.

They didn't need drums or torches to shoo away wild animals. However, about an hour before sunset,

Gajapati and his followers reached Simadri. The Administrator of Simadri, Sudarshan Dakshinakabata, had come a long way and camped to welcome Gajapati.

After the evening rituals for Jagannath, Dakshinakabata called a confidential meeting. It was planned at Sudarshan's behest. All the assembled Mahapatras, Champati or Chhamupati, a title given to a small landlord or small military commander and Bahinipatis, a commander of large military units, were to take a vow for integrity to boost Gajapati's spirit. A lot of commotions are taking place in Odisha. Many princes in Royal families are agitated in supporting Hamvira Deva's claim to the throne; as Hamvira Deva is a skilful warrior, many soldiers and Generals in each section of the army are on his side. Hence, the possibility of an organized opposition to the authority has been secretly fermenting to take the final shape of an armed revolt. It has gone to the public domain by now.

About one hour and a half after sundown at Fort Simadri, in the torchlight around the Fort, the dense green forests went into a deep slumber under the starry sky. Military guards patrolled with spears. Dakshinakabata thought even this cordon of guards needed to be increased. He asked the home guard to seal all the doors and windows of the conference hall. Two guards were at the open sides of the entrances so that no one from outside could eavesdrop on the discussions going on inside.

Sudarshan Dakshinakabata was Gajapati's relative.

In some way, Gajapati could not come to Simadri for the first ten years of his reign. *Matta* Bhanudev spent a few days in Simadri. Rajamahendriy's Reddy rulers let Vijayanagara occupy coastal regions and then captured Simadri Fort. Gangaraj Banudev could do nothing but back out into the hinterland of Odisha.

When Kapilendra Deva ascended the throne, *Matta* Bhanudev was hiding in Gudari-Katak. Kapilendra Deva encountered a civil war disturbance because the Odadi family neither accepted his authority nor paid the taxes. After eight long years of efforts and threats of confiscation, Kapilendra Deva could recapture all those regions. Kapilendra Deva realized that one's kin and kin were necessary for smooth and effective administration. "That is why, be it Khemundi or Rajamahendri, Simadri or Kondavidu if my blood relations are posted, we will face no betrayal of the kingdom's integrity. There would be no chances of ingratitude or treachery. No external enemy could secretly penetrate the Forts of Odisha," he decided.

In the presence of Gajapati and all the officials, Sudarshan Dakshinakabata began his welcome address.

"I welcome *Sri Sri Sri Gajapati – Gaudeshwar – Navakoti – Karnata – Kalabargeswar -Veeradhiveerabara Sri Sri Sri Kapilendra Deva* into this conference hall. When the last part of the Ganga regime bit the dust through, at some auspicious moment, Your Majesty took up the reins, and your lifelong conquests everywhere shaped this greater Odisha of today. Every inch of its land, Your Majesty, has been acquired by the willing martyrdom of Odia soldiers. Odisha was destined to have this. Your Majesty has spent all your life on battle fronts, but now, for family feuds, Your Majesty has lost peace of mind. At this critical juncture, not to speak of Simadri Fort, but all the subjects, royal officials, and the military extend their support and sympathy and pray that the blessings of the Lord Jagannath ward off all dangers.

It seems Gajapati's sad face glistened with joy. He began, "All the colleagues and Paika soldiers of Odisha, today I feel that this Simadri alone is the Southern capital of Odisha. The excellence of Odia infantry, cavalry, elephant corps and archers owes its magnificence to their training on this battlefield. This extended kingdom part is the same distance from the centre as Cuttack. There was a time when Simadri was outside our boundaries. Now we have acquired it, Odisha has spread beyond Simadri. At the slightest provocation, our powerful elephant corps will be present in action in no time. We needn't fear the enemy since we have a military base at Simadri.

"Today, I'm happy for one crucial reason. As and when the danger kept knocking at the door of Simadri, the king of Odisha had always rushed here. All Expeditions to the South began from here. Many military forces assume charge here. They play the role of a leaping tiger in the Aguani Thata. Taking this cue,

Narasimha Deva had come here and strengthened its structure. We know that before Narasimha Deva, his grandfather, Chodaganga Deva, was also touring here to inspect his kingdom sprawling from Ganga to Godavari.

"Narasimha Deva's pressure on the South was tremendous. He used to stay back at Simadri but, if needed, was marching to Gajapati's Fort, which was close to Vijayawada. He eyed further South, too. When Konark temple was under construction, he had erected a Lakshmi Narayana Temple at Simadri simultaneously.

"But disaster struck during *Matta* Bhanudev's reign. Since Gangaraj closed his eyes to the Odisha boundary, Dev Ray, the king of Vijayanagara, captured coastal tracts. Of course, he had yet to catch Simadri. Gangaraj was thinking about how to regain Kalinga Dandapata that extended up to Rajamahendry in the original Odisha map, and all that daydream came to him sitting at Simadri. Finally, Rajamahendri ruler AleyaBhima Reddy occupied Simadri and drove Gangaraj to Gudari-Katak of Paralakhemundi. From there, he never returned to his capital, Bidanasi Cuttack, for the painful emotion of shame.

The Ganga dynasty continued for four hundred years. As short-sighted Ganga kings lacked the spirit of aggrandizement, Odisha lost its southern part. To regain a military centre like Simadri, I had to use a lot of my mind. The enemy wasn't confined to Rajamahendry only; its support base extended to Dev Ray, the king of Vijayanagara. After we captured it, God helped us conquer Rajamahendry without difficulty. Time presented favourable circumstances for us only after Dev Ray's power decline in Vijayanagara.

And during the last few years, our authority in Telangana areas increased. Many strongholds fell to our forces, and we put them under Simadri's administration. This extensive territory not only increased our revenue but also increased our military power and administrative responsibilities manifold. We deployed a vast army here and renovated it to make it more impregnable.

"But Muslim invasions and Vijayanagara's greed were focussed on this Fort. A solid idea came to my mind to protect every chamber of the fortress, including the southern treasury. The weakest part of a house is its entrance door. No force could break it down if we prepare it in brass or especially bell bronze. If this metallic door is painted grey, it won't look like a bell metal door, which would misguide the visual estimation of the enemy.

"It won't be an exaggeration if this southern military headquarters of Odisha is called the second Katak. With the proliferation of Muslim invasions and faced with the mighty Vijayanagara Empire, guarding the borders of a large kingdom like Odisha seemed to be an impossible task. If Vijayanagara invaded from the South, irrespective of the size and strength of the

Odisha army, reaching the southern part of Simadri from Bidanasi Cuttack would take not less than seven days. But by then, the enemy might have occupied the border territory."

Gajapati paused for a while.

Antaranga Mahapatra was thinking about Gajapati's past. Indeed, one day, he failed to penetrate this Fort. How to establish himself as a real winner was a challenge for him. When so many feudatories were against the new Gajapati, how could Gangaraj's relatives cooperate with the Odisha administration? After long cogitation, Kapilendra Deva hit upon a plan. It was to enhance his military capabilities that would surely subjugate neighbouring kingdoms, not to speak of feudal chiefs. This strategy was Kapilendra Deva's only way left. All of them knew that, but it was not easy. He was using all his energy and time on the strength of his prodigious patience. He toured feudatories and hill areas where the native population eagerly awaited to render military service. He recruited healthy, non-disabled men for the army from villages of Odisha. He maintained top priority to this during his reign. He warned the refractory feudal chiefs who incited sabotage in the kingdom. One day, frightened by this, Odadi surrendered. After that, he turned Simadri into a second military base."

Gajapati's words were softer after speaking out on his past glory with trembling lips, although he felt pain in his heart. He resumed, "All days are not the same regarding what happens. I wonder today about how I could ever do such remarkable jobs in the past, for example, the brass door here at Simadri Fort. How could it come to my mind? Wood breaks like earthenware, but brass is hard and strong, so I ordered to install a bell bronze gateway specially made for the purpose.

"Today, that brass door-like defence strategy has broken due to family feuds. When wood becomes hollow, it breaks itself; why should anyone break it? The Lord's wishes must be fulfilled; who am I to work against it? Whenever any unforeseen obstacle comes, the Lord takes care of it."

With these words, he returned to the temple of Jagannath again. It looked as if he lay prostrate before Him to pray for divine favour.

Just then, *Purohita* Mahapatra stood near him. He had a word of consolation, "We must do what the Lord ordained. What He needs through us is revealed itself in dreams."

After Gajapati thought for a moment, there was a streak of a smile on his face. The Lord's blessings, He hasn't uttered, but they found expression in *Purohita* Mahapatra's words. He has obeyed the revelation in his dream and chosen his heir. Everyone cannot take it that way. His servant, the Mahapatra, conveyed the decree of the Lord.

Simadri is like another Purushottama Kshetra.

Lord Jagannath oversees the South from here. The people in the southern territory consider Fort Simadri symbolic of the Lord's omnipotence. The Lord's power rests here; it can solve the religious crisis in the South of Bharatavarsha by liquidating Muslim power.

Kapilendra Deva was introspective. Why did the people of southern Hindu kingdoms seek the power of Gajapati? Was it simply the spiritual association of Lord Jagannath? He has already announced himself to be the Lord's servant. Again, all the Gajapati army's might is with the Lord's blessings. The Lord alone has charmed the people and is helping them invisibly.

Kapilendra has labelled himself as the Lord's servant only to retrieve the glory of the Lord. He could be Gajapati due to His blessings, so he has fixed the goal of his life to bring the all-around progress of Jagannath temple. He recalled an incident that happened seven years ago, in 1460 AD. He was elated at the series of victories in Telangana areas; he had the intuition that the Trinity of his motherland was leading him to conquer Fort after Fort. Paridhanas, the detachment of commanding officers and Fort duty officers in charge of the captured territory, had finished the collection of abundant quantities of jewellery. The treasurers were transporting the wealth acquired from defeated kingdoms to Fort Simadri.

Gajapati is in ecstasy in the fathomless depth of his mind. The kind of joy from that victory series seldom happens in one's life. He is racing through the interior of Telangana in limitless euphoria. Fort after Fort, the feudal chiefs surrendered and heaped their treasure before the Gajapati army. *Paridhanas* dispatched all the gems to treasury heads at Simadri Fort loaded on elephants.

Easy and convincing victory without bloodshed. Yet, an immense booty of wealth Kapilendra Deva did not expect. Now, he is comparing himself with his past self. He was not the hideous slayer of men like Sikandar of Greece. Sikandar was at the zenith of pride and arrogance, driven by dreams of world conquest, and had gone on genocide after the genocide in Persia and the neighbouring countries. He was also not Sultan Mahmoud, who plundered Somanath Temple time and again, carrying away immense wealth to his native place. Of course, he didn't know much about the supreme leader of Ekamra Kumarigiri, who spread dharma all over Bharatavarsha and could build that titanic kingdom of Kalinga. The king of Utkal had been consistently strong for his elephant corps. He wins every battle but never resorts to genocide. Why should he be reckless like Ashoka the Black? Human life is valuable, and with an elephant, troop victory was possible with no resistance and without much bloodshed and death.

This afternoon of Magha, equivalent to February in the Gregorian calendar, the city of Warangal, sculpted on a single rock, accepted Kapilendra Deva's suzerainty. Who could resist an army of two thousand elephants? Gajapati Kapilendra Deva visited idols of self-manifested Swayambhu Shiva and Lord Srirama installed in the Ramapa Temple there. His devotion for Jagannath emanated from the depths of his soul and filled him with exuberance. The Vaishnavite splendour of Lord Srirama illuminated him.

Suddenly, he felt the manifestation of Lord Jagannath, Balabhadra and Subhadra. Jagannath listens in his internal ear to a divine puzzled question, "Where will you store this copious wealth, Gajapati? Is there any space for it in your treasury?"

Kapilendra Deva's illusion snapped off. He once again glanced at Lord Srirama.

He is silent. Who put this problem before him?

"Yes, in fact, our Cuttack treasury runs short of space. My thirst for victory has no intention of stuffing my treasury to the choking point to satisfy myself. My victory chain will continue. This money is the income of the Gajapati armies. I cannot find time to build the Kruttibash temple or a thousand temples of Ekamra as the Somavamsi Kings of Odisha did. My military expeditions aim to smash surrounding kings and lessen the strength of enemies. It is my hereditary trait. My grandfather was a General in the military of Gangas. His leadership was invincible. My father was the leader of the elephantry unit. Their tenacious willpower always shows up in me. Kapilendra will continue to play this game of militarism.

"Kapilendra will never accept defeat. He will

certainly wait till the right moment arrives. Time offers chances, and victory is assured if we utilize them correctly. I have experienced it in my life not once but many times. Be it Rajamahendry Reddy, Bahamani Sultan, Sultan of Banga, or the Emperor of Vijayanagara, we could subdue them after I availed the optimum use of time and opportunities.

"Lord Jagannath, I am your servant, but what am I doing? Instead of answering your question politely, I boast of my victories and feel proud of myself. The fact is that you ordain all my successes. When Gajapati of Odisha goes to the South, he seeks your blessings and bows before you. Indeed, you have put into my elephantry the strength of a million lions. Each victory of mine is backed and energized by your vigilant eyes.

"Your heavenly form encourages me manifold. I shall carry in my heart your auspicious image adorned with a few of the ornaments. You are the perfectly embellished Trinity of mine. I wish to see your divine face whenever I am on my way back from the conquests. My Simadri treasurer is preparing some ornaments, especially for you, which will be carried to Puri to enrich Your Ratna Bhandar."

At that time *Purohita* Mahapatra looked at Gajapati. A reasoning flashed in his mind: whether Gajapati was unstable psychologically. *Purohita* Mahapatra lost no more time as Gajapati's daydream ended abruptly. *Purohita* Mohapatra dazzled with his eloquence, "Your Majesty, with the blessings of

Jayadurga, when you dedicated that gold jewellery loaded on sixteen war elephants for Jagannath temple, we had a hint of your great heart suffused in frenzied devotion. Your Majesty's highly devoted life will spiritually be fulfilled by adorning the idols with gold. But noticing your zeal, servitor *Badatadau* prayed to you that the general public can't see all the ritual embellishments of the Lord on the bejewelled throne. So he requested you to reperform the ritual of openly dressing the Lod in gold on the chariot in the last phase of the car festival.

Since then, Your Majesty has made 138 types of golden ornaments studded with gemstones to adorn the idols in a delightful appearance on the chariot on *Bada Ekadasi*. With Lord Jagannath's grace, you have gone all the way to make this Neelachal Dham attractive. Meghanad and Kurum Pacheri, the high outer walls of the Lord's temple, are the masterpieces of your imagination. The Lord's *Chandan Jatra* and display in lake water or *chapa-khela* were not there before. Your divine inspiration had started those celebrations. Many other cultural practices have also been Your Majesty's contribution. The Trinity's visit to the Mausima temple on Car Festival and mother Lakshmi's rage and return clutching a few pieces of a log from the vimana on the *Herapanchami* day are ritual aspects of your deep thought.

"Your mystery doesn't end with it. On the day of the Car Festival, your sympathetic heart melted for Mother Lakshmi when Jagannath and Balabhadra asked her to guard the home and then went to Mausima's house. You are the stage manager of all the live acts we see on *Herapanchami*. On this day, devotees get ample opportunity to know many facts associated with you and realize your greatness when they see the golden idols gifted by you. All of Purushottam is Your Majesty's extended family.

Before this, after winning "MalikaParisa" of Banga, you offered the *'Pundarika Gopa'* saree to Jagannath. Your Majesty's military conquests bathed Lord Purushottam and Jagannath temple ecstatically as if those ancient Trinity were participants in your battles against the enemy."

A flicker of a smile began spreading on the face of the Gajapati, signalling the pleasure felt in his heart.

A little ripple of a smile played on Gajapati's face. But many in the public laughed away or dismissed with contempt the dream revelation of who should be chosen heir to the throne. Still, Jagannath alone knows why He didn't walk on the beaten track and decided to be an unlikely candidate for the same. Gajapati has given top priority to the Lord in all his works, whether in the capacity of a father or a General in battle. Whatever the Lord has ordained, he has accepted.

That night, Gajapati walked to the bedroom. Mahapatras, too, departed to their respective bedrooms. Each of them wanted much-needed sleep.

The following day, there was the schedule of receiving a guard of honour from the forces deployed at Simadri. Kapilendra Deva was a warrior. Despite troubled circumstances, he would undoubtedly receive a guard of recognition from the resident parties of every stronghold. The military chief of Simadri Fort Ratnakar Pahadsingh has prepared a short play in honour of Gajapati's presence.

It was the morning of Margasira month. The intensity of the cold hadn't subsided. Gajapati's daily habit in his military career was to exercise briefly in the early hours, a little before sunrise, and do a bit of jogging. Still, on the day of the military guard of honour, Ratnakar Pahadasingh led him to the Simadri military training fields. Antaranga Mahapatra also accompanied them. Other Mahapatras followed suit.

The arrangement was there at short notice in that extensive arena. Odia Paika soldiers assembled in full military gear, And they were excited with the rising warmth of their blood to the marching tune of Odisha war trumpets. With the trumpets was the frenzied cacophony of war drums, victory drums, and Ranasingha that usually are maddeningly exciting for soldiers on the battlefield.

Gajapati, riding a light yellow-hued horse in this belligerent atmosphere, inspected the guard of honour.

After the war trumpets scene, Gajapati was

seated on the dais. The soldiers began to be in battle array. Like on the battlefield, the soldiers split into two groups and stood face to face with their weapons ready.

The loudness of war drums decreased after creating the hot atmosphere of a battlefield. Then military chief Pahadsingh spoke out, "I prostrate before Your Majesty Sri Sri Sri... Gajapati- Gaudeshwar-Navakoti-Karnatakala-Bargeswar-Biradhibirabara-Kapilendra Deva, who is present among us and seated on the dais, and offer my salutations Your Majesty has elevated our spirit and boasted up our morale and has engendered Odia militarism. Although Odia militarism never had in the past any legendary accomplishments to its credit, now the arms and ammunitions of our forces, our black elephant corps, war horses, and at the root of all, the daredevilry of our Paika fighters testify adequately to our military superiority.

When, at one time, Yavan rulers were going to occupy Odisha from the north and South, Gajapati Kapilendra Deva emerged from the Kruttibash Temple of Ekamra. Of course, last, Gangaraj *Matta* Bhanudev welcomed him as he was down by anarchic elements. Gangaraj from Gudari-Katak must have realized all the progress the kingdom was making.

At such a juncture, as Gajapati-Gaudeshwar out to restore Odia forces, he also raised the honour of the Odisha kingdom, Odia language and Odia culture.

In every aspect of governance, the Odisha of today has been honoured as the foremost kingdom in the country. It has a single most crucial reason. That is the warmth of Odia's blood, Odia Paika's temperament and above all, the caring attitude of its rulers.

Today, Odia Paika is heavily armed, and Odia's mindset prefers honour and self-esteem. There was a time when outside forces tried to use the surrender attitude to their advantage. Their hungry eyes rested on the treasury of jewels and gems and the Lord of Lords, Jagannath, the heartthrob of Odisha. If Odisha people lose their courage, they will lose everything. In this critical juncture, our motherland has begotten the warrior of warriors, Gajapati Kapilendra, whose Highness had acquired innumerable titles for his series of victories.

Shall I say a few words about who is His Majesty's ideal? Do you know what his ideal is? Two personalities influenced him. One of these is Narasimha Deva of the powerful Ganga dynasty. Narasimha was a lion in human appearance. Many Odishan kings were simply defensive, resisting as and when Bengal Muslim kings attacked. But Narasimha was aggressive, pounced on them and defeated them. Narasimha Deva assumed the title of Gajapati because of the elephant corps he had formed and got it inscribed on Kapilash stone inscriptions. Kapilendra used the word 'Gajapati' for him. He has built himself as the most successful Gajapati and also has been fond of the title.

He has also used the elephant force successfully to accomplish the impossible. He has justified the naming of his Suryavamsa as the Gajapati dynasty. He can foresee the bright feeling of the dynasty's future.

The second legendary character that makes inspirational waves in his mind is the invincible Kharavela of Ekamra Kumarigiri. We feel that our emperor was the conqueror of Bharatavarsha, as engraved in the stone sculptures of Kumarigiri caves. He laid the foundation stone for the series of victories by Kalinga with its countless elephants, horses and chariots. He proved to the world that Kalinga is synonymous with bravery. To justify this commendation should be the goal of every son of our soil.

Our king is the worthy son of a warrior family. Fighting battles is his family's occupation. He spent his life in battles. Even the Mahabharata battle lasted a little less than eighteen days. Our Gajapati's war period is more than thirty-two years. Hats off to his courage and perseverance; hats off to his accomplishments. Even in this ripe old age, his blood is youthful. He is high-minded ambitious, and has built Odisha in his image, so he was born "the Odisha nation." Our mother tongue we accept as our beloved 'Odia language', and the Odia gold coin 'Pagoda' was circulated as a mark of our proud independence in economic matters.

The country was under spiralling Afghan-Turkish invasions for two hundred years after Gangaraj

Narasimha Deva, Odisha's army, could amass strength; this created a dangerous situation. Whoever was the ruler of Odisha, if he moved southward, he had to face Bengal Nawab's onslaughts from behind; if northward he went, Bahamani or Vijayanagara armies were there, and it had become a daily routine for them to cross the Odisha border. Even the Muslim Nawab of faraway Jaunpur was also biding his time to capture Odisha.

The moment His Majesty ascended the throne, internal bickering ballooned into a gigantic shape. Despite this, he was in search of a military base. He worked hard in his mind to frame rules regarding his forces, armaments, elephantry, cavalry and various other military gadgets. Likewise, regulations for each feudatory suitable for their capacity and capabilities were in place. He also decided approximately what share of expenses they would have to defray and to what extent they would cooperate with Gajapati during the kingdom's defence or military campaigns. The result: Odisha upsurged once again as a military superpower. Odisha developed its intelligence network and waited for an opportunity. Destiny and chance came to his aid, and Gajapati, the Crest Jewel, accomplished building his strength.

His military strategies, at his time, were that of a genius. The tactics were innovative. With sound military espionage, he was finding a window of operation. From his experience, he reorganized the

Odia Paika force. Its modus operandi was different from that of other regions. Patriotic inspiration and complete submission to Lord Jagannath can energize you, which was his motivation for Odia forces. Structurally, Odia Thata appeared in its new avatar, Dalabehera, as the chief of a group of 27 Paikas. A skilful Paikaray would head a group of 70 Paikas, the group being called a Bhuyan. Many Bhuyans formed a Bahini under a Bahinipati. When we count all Bahinis together, it is called a Chhamu, of which the chief was Chhamupati or Champati. Generally, cavalrymen were designated Raut and their leader, Rautray.

Similarly, the head of the elephantry was Sahani. Countless Odia soldiers were enrolled in the Thatas and kept not only Odisha but the whole of Bharatvarsha lively and pulsating.

In any military campaign, work is in progress, and the apportionment of work is according to hierarchy. So Chhamu had many divisions: the Hantakaru Thata cleaning up the way, then Aguani Thata actual fighting forces, Pachhiani Thata or soldiers guarding the king and the commander from the rear, and Paridhana Thata in charge of the captured forts. In this way, the military force was not one compact group or an army moving only in one direction. Gajapati could simultaneously campaign in the South and drive out Muslim forces in distant northern territories. From the time of Gajapati, Mandaran and Kurumbedha Forts were ready to work like shields for Odisha.

Merit alone finds merit. Kapilendra first identified the regions where people supported joining the forces and the areas where recruitment to the military was significant. Then, he planned to enlist the army using very minute methods. Skilful foot soldiers, cavalrymen and elephant-mounting soldiers of such areas who had shown exceptional fighting skill on the battlefield were identified by touring every village. Then he conferred on them titles such as Dandasena, Dandapata, Dandanayak, Paschimakabat, Dakshinakabata, Samantaray, Bidyadhara, Baliarsingha, Pahadasingh, Gadanayak, Jena, Badajena, Parichha, Paribas, Pratihari, Dandapani, Samal, Nayak,

Pradhan, thereby awakening in them a new heartthrob of liveliness and self-esteem to be part of the army.

Pahadasingh of Fort Simadri, by his farsight, conjectured, "In today's world, it's not an exaggeration to say that the Gajapati style military is important in the whole world. The zeal in each home to join the forces and the spirited welcome accorded to Paikas in all the villages are expanding Odia's militarism and the size of the Paika army. Indeed, Odia Paika stood up to all the examples of courage and bravery witnessed worldwide."

After narrating the fundamentals of Odia militarism in this way, Pahadasingh noticed at Gajapati. Gajapati's whole-hearted response inspired him to move to the next programme.

He continued, "Right now, Bahamani and Malwa are decisively defeated forces Banga and Jaunpur Nawabs have lost their teeth after just a single battle against us. These Yavans will never again muster the courage to look at Odisha or its treasury. We will deal with Vijayanagara last.

However, let's see how our Gajapati forces from the South are pouncing on Saluva Narasimha of Vijayanagara, who is camping in the South.

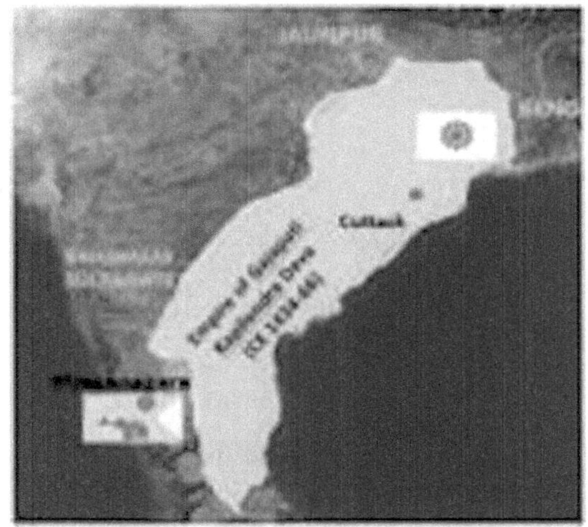
Gajapati's Expeditions

Indeed, a shadow dance on the war theme began.

Gajapati restfully enjoyed the show. When Odisha is commanding Kondavidu, what can Vijayanagara do?

Gajapati felt that Odia Paika had retained his uniqueness. This much is enough to keep the enemy at bay.

If ever he has done something for Odisha, it is this militarism and formation of power centres in every village.

Gajapati has explored and framed all possible strategies for restoring Odia's self-consciousness and self-esteem.

He returned from the army training centre to the Fort. He imparted practical motivation to the army. Bravery in battle is his life; skilful manoeuvre is his breath. At his young age, only he could build the Odisha kingdom. A bright future glittered before his eyes.

About two days later, he passed while resting at Simadri Fort. Gajapati realized he must move to Kondavidu for urgent work. The sooner he reached there, the better.

He decided he would depart from Simadri early next morning for Rajamahendry.

Anekapalli Stronghold

(*Anakapalli of today*)

Rajahmundry is a long distance from Simadri Fort. Still, Odia military campsites and rest houses were there at definite intervals. The royal journey was safe and well-guarded without any difficulty. This route is the ordinary roadway from Cuttack to Rajamahendry. You move along a few miles, and you are welcome in.

On top of this, Gajapati Kapilendra Deva was touring the South on some urgent mission. So Odia army was alert all along the route.

After covering about twelve miles from Simadri, Gajapati halted at Visakhapatnam for breakfast. After that, he reached Anekapalli only in one hour and a half. The Odia resident forces were in a fort only twenty miles ahead.

"Here we break the journey for the night," Gajapati said, "This Anekapalli fort is a prestigious one for the royal line of Gajapati."

The in-charge of the Fort led the royal entourage honourably inside. Gajapati, marching southward, has arrived at the Fort before sunset. After the day ended, the tour to Rajamahendry Dandapata would be challenging. Rivers and creeks would be on the way to slow down movement. So departure in the early hour of the morning would be convenient.

During the vacation, Antaranga Mahapatra told Gajapati, "Your Majesty, we will lose our speed on the way; I am afraid someone is going to block our way."

Gajapati replied, "Antaranga, you have accompanied me on this route several times. Can you say when we bypassed Anekapalli? Whatever the urgency of work making us go south or north, we stayed only here for rest. This place has a special attraction."

The Mahapatras said in a chorus," This Fort is different from others. It has neither an outer wall nor a compound. It is fully open and has the look of a village. What speciality it has such that Gajapati is bound to stay in the open?"

Antaranga Mahapatra, "It is already evening. First, let's finish the ritual offering of holy evening prayer to Lord Jagannath; then, we shall discuss it awhile in the meeting hall."

"This is a place for maintaining good public relations because many villages are around. Those villagers will spread the news that Gajapati is arriving, and a large crowd will gather around us. They take Gajapati to be one among them. They are thrilled at Gajapati's conquests. "

After the ritual, *Purohita* Mahapatra, Gajapati and other Mahapatras assembled in the hall. The royal gatekeeper of Anekapalli informed villagers that he had arrived to meet Gajapati. They were about two hundred strong, but seven village heads were among them.

Just then, Antaranga Mahapatra talked with the gatekeeper secretly regarding Gajapati's security. He felt relieved and wondered how this kind of tight security could be in place, although Gajapati's arrival was entirely unexpected, and Odisha military forces had no knowledge of it.

At this time, *Sandhibigraha* Mahapatra came to Gajapati and prayed to him, muffled, "Your Majesty, seven Anekapalli heads have come to seek your audience. The people assembled with them also wanted to glimpse the Gajapati, Jagannath's representative."

Gajapati was involved with Anekapalli all his life. He was acquainted with Anekapalli at least ten years before he became Gajapati. During his movement to and fro via this route, the seven heads of the nearby seven villages joined him in the meeting hall, discussed sundry matters and prayed to him for public facilities as if they were his kin.

Although daylight faded, several torches illuminated the open field before the gate. Old Gajapati appeared before the crowd, waiting to see him. When they all saluted him, it was as if they were hailing the Lord, touching His feet. Even though Jagannath was in Puri, He fused Himself with Gajapati, making him the living God Jagannath, the deity manifested in human form. All those gathered there saluted Gajapati, bending before him, and begged for his blessings.

Gajapati said, "All of you Anekapalli villagers think I'm one of your kin, and that's my good fortune. Even at this age, my memory is still strong. What I remember about forty to forty-five years ago, I had to spend one day and one night in your village. I had an urgent call from Rajamahendry Fort. Gangapati Bhanudev had sent me from Cuttack to discuss Odisha and Vengirajya border issue. The Nawab from afar was waiting for me. But it was impossible to move forward on horseback beyond Anekapalli due to the torrential rain. Nearby Sarada River flooded with untimely rainwater that winter and threatened to overflow. At first, the villagers took fright looking at our fifty cavalrymen. However, the sight of our flag assured them. Then they arranged for our accommodation. I can't just forget that night because of your unsolicited hospitality. You created a highly cordial relationship between you and me. Your respectful love and natural affection for me made me feel like Anekapalli was a divine shelter. The reason is that by daybreak, the river had become a lean stream of water, thus enabling us to reach Rajamahendry in time; thereby, we could negotiate to avoid confrontation on the border. "

Then *Sandhibigraha* Mahapatra said, "This village of yours is an inseparable part of Odisha. Its heritage goes back long into the past. Excellent folklore and sculptural relics also show this village was under the Chedi rulers one thousand five hundred years ago. Now, the seven heads of the seven villages may come into the meeting hall to exchange a few words with Gajapati."

The crowd of Anekapalli assembled there felt that Gajapati's unexpected tour southward and his company was a matter of great luck for them, and so felt highly gratified. Some grizzly old village Nayakas could recall that about forty-five years ago, one day, they had extended hospitality to General Kapil Raut as a royal guest. That same General is so fortunate and industrious that he today is the mighty Gajapati and the creator of indivisible Odisha. This Anekapalli was as thrilled at each of his victories as it throbbed with each of his efforts. It is a fact that from the first experience itself, he thinks of Anekapalli as the harbinger of good luck. On the occasion of every campaign to the South, he touched the villages and their people, maybe for a few moments, and when he departed with the victory flag fluttering, it created an air of ecstasy. Then there was that unheard chanting, "Son of mother Odisha has won, has captured Forts, has added to the territory of our motherland", rending the air.

Who excited him for all that daredevilry with risk to his life? Indeed, it was not for him. To earn a living in his native place, he never needed ancestral wealth. He endangered his own life to face formidable enemies; he was passionate about sacrificing thousands of his subjects and innumerable horses and elephants with other livestock. Was all that for his pleasure? This Kapil Raut Dalapati strongly desired to pray to the mother goddess he held in his heart. He achieved it. He is not a resident of Anekapalli, but the villagers there consider him as one among them. They were tenacious and often went to Bidanasi Cuttack to glimpse Gajapati. They got affection in ample measure from him.

Gajapati extended help to Anekapalli unhesitatingly. Simultaneously with the Kapileswar Kapilanath Shaiva Kshetra temple of Ekamra, many Shiva temples were built at Anekapalli through God's grace. Many of the deepest Lingas had come up here, tearing the earth. Many Shiva temples have ponds and pools dug beside them.

Upon receipt of the news that River Sarada had created havoc, Gajapati Kapilendra Deva helped them in all ways, from repairing the river banks to rehabilitating the people.

Now *Sandhibigraha* Mahapatra informed, "All of you have met Gajapati. Gajapati would talk to your seven *Nayakas,* the village chiefs to discuss your village affairs. As you think him to be your kin, he too thinks so."

The Nayakas expressed their gratitude to Gajapati and said, "Your Majesty, you donated a considerable amount to our stone deity emerging out of netherworlds, the *Patalaphuta Linga* from below. We constructed our Shiva Temple. Now rituals are going on there in full steam. Five years have passed in the meantime. But is Your Majesty not going to the South? You have not put your foot even once in our village."

"No, my tours to the South have significantly decreased due to domestic problems. Otherwise, as you all know, this is the passage I always frequent, and your village is my regular resting place. I always use this route. Onward when I go, and on my return journey, this is where evening descends. Anekapalli, hence, is my favourite place. "

Sambhu Nayak of Pahadasahi was a bit chatty and, of all *Nayakas*, the more experienced and with a reasonable leadership quality. He courageously told Gajapati, "All of us Anekapalli villagers are thrilled at Gajapati's conquests in the South. Everybody was happy with a big Odisha stretching up to Kanya Kumari. Let God give you a long life, for you have protected our temple from the butchers. The elephantry of Gajapati is roaming in the South. Wherever it finds injustice and oppression, it shows its enormous strength to restore justice. Social justice is the virtue of Gajapati Maharaj and Lord Jagannath's glory. "

Gajapati heard Sambhu Nayak's words attentively.

Again, Shambhu began, "Even in your absence in the South, Gajapati forces are ready for any eventuality. Your son Hamvira Deva Mahapatra is invincible. He has the courage of a hundred tuskers. We saw him five years ago. When the Gajapati army was invading the Bahamani capital at Bidar, and the father returned to the northern border, passing through our land to check the infiltration of Jaunpur Nawab, did the prince stay back? He proved his strength and courage by conquering kingdom after kingdom. Thanks to such a father who sired such a virtuous son. He subdued the whole South and let Odisha's flag flutter everywhere.

Sandhibigraha Mahapatra stopped him lest he should speak further. He asked them to put forth their grievances, if any. He informed Gajapati that he must depart for Rajamahendry early in the morning.

But the *Nayaks* didn't say anything and departed with bowed heads.

Gajapati could not withstand the pain associated with the utterance of Hamvira Deva's name. He looked sad. He became absent-minded. Nowadays, he is irritated to hear about the glory of Hamvira Deva. He suspected that his Hamvira Deva could not be a simple man. Despite being a descendant of the Gajapati dynasty, who can say that one day he would not join with Bahamani or some other Yavan ruler to carry out an organized revolt against Odisha? What guarantee is there that parts of Odisha will not be affected?

Gajapati Kapilendra Deva drew pensive with Hamvira Deva's topic. Hamvira Deva was no disinherited son. He was his highly skilled warrior son. His bravery was extraordinary. He needn't brood so much. It's okay if he managed the whole southern part of Odisha as its governor. If he is addicted to becoming Gajapati, problems will arise.

A relaxing Gajapati

Ile-Majhili on Rajamahendry Route

Gajapati Kapilendra Deva's journey from Cuttack to Kondapalli was a significant undertaking, and is Mahapatras made every effort to ensure his comfort and well-being during the trip. Despite their best efforts, it's natural to assume that an elderly Gajapati might have experienced some fatigue during the journey. The exact number of times Gajapati had travelled this route was not counted, but it's clear that he had undertaken numerous campaigns and military expeditions to the south throughout his reign as Gajapati.

Gajapati's travels and military campaigns often required him to move between the northern and southern borders of Odisha. For example, the preparation by Jaunabad Nawab and attacks on Mandaran Fort by Banga Nawab in the north might have forced him to change his plans and retreat to the northern border. Such strategic shifts were not uncommon for a ruler like Gajapati, and his movements were generally coordinated by the Gajapati Army, including schedules for rest and night halts.

This time, on urgent military and administrative grounds, he is touring with six Mahapatras on horseback and is moving without much sleep. Regarding where he will have lunch and where he will stay for the night, it's common knowledge that Gajapati certainly has his preferences.

In two days, Gajapati's army arrived at Ile-majhile village. For some reason, this was also his favourite place. He has a Gajapati palace there. He also had many known village heads, as was in Anekapalli. The evening may be one hour and a half away. Much before the sun kissed the western horizon, they had reached the Majhili village.

Gajapati could notice many village heads he had known for at least two decades. This village was considerable, but the villagers have become disappointed with paying taxes continuously for ages. In the beginning itself, they complained to Gajapati. At that point, Kapilendra Deva was mustering all his strength to dislodge the Reddys from Rajamahendry. The last Ganga king, Bhanudev, lost the throne due to this. But Kapilendra Deva could capture Rajamahendry after fourteen years of his accession. The new Gajapati campaigned south with his elephantry and defeated the Reddys. On hearing this, the joy of Majhili villagers knew no bounds. They were finally at peace.

On his way back, Gajapati granted them some concessions, for which they expressed gratitude. The villagers vented their grievances, "Your Majesty, we are often troubled because of our peculiar location. We belong to Kalinga Dandapata and so belong to Odisha. But when Odisha becomes weak, southern powers capture us. Our village is right on the common border; both sides demand tax payments from us. We pray you to consider this fact and decide something for our deliverance. Dual control and tax payment are problems remaining unsolved for long."

Before Gajapati said something, *Sandhibigraha* Mahapatra intervened, "Please hear me. The Kalinga border stretches from Bhagirathi Ganga in the North to the holy river Godavari in the South, Kalinga Sagar and the sea in the East and Amarakantak in the West. The strength of Kalinga, or today's Odisha, has grown during the reign of the Chedi dynasty, or Mahameghavahana Kharavela, of Gangaraj Chodaganga Devaa and Narasimha Deva. Of course, sometimes our might is not visible due to family fights when our forces appear weak from the outside. And then southern neighbouring forces enter the borders. The result: villages on the border suffer."

Gajapati has now assured them that no external enemy will trouble them anymore. Yet Odisha will be their saviour to guard them against the enemy. In addition, this region is declared tax-free.

This assurance dates back to seventeen years ago.

Now, the people of that village, Majhili, have gathered to welcome Gajapati. He is not in his former designation; his powers have increased. He is the emperor of the gigantic Gajapati Empire. Its boundaries have extended far and wide. Majhili is no longer sitting on the border. It is well inside Odisha territory today. Odisha has grown up to Kanyakumari, which is its southern boundary now.

Fort under Expeditious Odisha

Gajapati's southbound forces reached Ile-Majhili at noon. Gajapati and Mahapatras rested there for a while. At that time, the crowd garlanded him and rent the air with their joyous ululations.

Some important people of the village met Gajapati after his rest. They thanked him for his benevolent rule over them and said, "Your Majesty, Yavan forces have accepted defeat. The power that was going to commit many vicious deeds against our customs and practices your elephantry has pushed back them. When enemy power attacks Gajapati, the whole of the South strongly feels the gloom, not Majhili village alone. Gajapati himself is the living embodiment of Lord Jagannath. Odisha administration is pious and sympathetic to the subjects.

"Concerning Odisha administration, the subjects of the Gajapati Empire always pray to Jagannath for his protection and for Gajapati's victory at all times, to be free from the inhuman governance of the growing Bahamani force. Indeed, Odia soldiers are very much orthodox and pious. They work against injustice and oppression. They work based on humanism.

"Gajapati has toured after a long time. All strongholds have come under Gajapati's rule. Your virtuous son Hamvira Deva is in the South. Apart from the honour he gets as the son of Gajapati, he has generated such a strong attraction in the heart of every man in the South by his strength, courage and generalship, as it is just unbelievable. The enemy breaks up and hides when it hears Prince Hamvira Deva is coming. On the other hand, the general public rejoice, and the whole area reverberates with celebrations.

"Besides, Gajapati's third generation Hamvira Deva's noble son Kapileswar Kumar is Parichha of Kondavidu. It tantamounts to the expansion of Gajapati hegemony and propagation of the Jagannath cult. People believe that Sri Jagannath is spreading His glory throughout the South of Bharatavarsha. "

Hamvira Deva's Telengana Fight

Praise on the prince pained Gajapati. He kept quiet. He acknowledged all the achievements of Hamvira Deva. But he could not speak in his favour. He wanted to crown Purushottam Dev as his successor and retire from regal responsibilities himself. The crowning of Purusottama is what Lord Jagannath wants. And since he is a servant of Lord Jagannath, how can he go against it?

Despite Hamvira Deva's strength and brilliance, as long as the Lord doesn't want it, Kapilendra Deva can't declare him his successor. Of course, he is not unwilling to hand over the charge of the southern portion of the country to his virtuous son by exercising his powers as a ruler.

Gajapati sighed, indicating exacerbation and relief, and said, "Let's not delay our journey."

At that time, *Sandhibigraha* Mahapatra said, "Your Majesty, These areas were in the control of Odisha. Although these tracts seceded during Ganga rule, the love and respect of the people for Gajapati remained intact. The rise of Gajapati in Odisha has made them hopeful of freedom from Yavan subjugation and cruelty. Lord Jagannath was going with Gajapati from Puri, but He had confined himself to the territorial limits of a contracted Odisha. Now, He will be present in the expanded Odisha. Everyone in the remote area of our kingdom will now feel the mystical power of Purushottam Puri.

Statue of Gajapati

Rajamahendry Fort

Reaching Rajamahendry was not too late. They arrived at Pithapur, a stone's throw distance from Rajamahendry. Out of curiosity, Gajapati asked his Mahapatras, "Do you see any trace of the effect of Odia language here?"

Antaranga Mahapatra replied, "Your Majesty, this 'Pithapur' word is an Odia word, not of Telugu or Sanskrit origin. We Odias call it so, but the locals use Pithapuram or the old name Peethikapuram instead.

Sandhibigraha Mahapatra, more knowledgeable about sundry matters, began to speak, "This Pithapur is a seat of God and the centre of divine energy (Saktipeetha). Lord Kukuteswar Swami is the deity of this Shaivapitha. Legend has it that he was born from Mother Saraswati's left hand. It is an ancient Saktipeetha known as Dakshina Kasi. Since it is part of Odisha, we might have altered the Telugu name to Pithapur to suit us. For ages, Godavari Bank has been on the boundary of Odisha. We take it to be our southern border. It's a safe guess that under the stewardship of Ganga kings such as Chodaganga and Narasimha Deva, Odia language dominated this region."

Gajapati felt a big crowd was expecting him at Pithapur. As things turned out, Rajamahendry was only some ten miles away when he found Parichha, the administrator of that area, had come to welcome him accompanied by many Odia Paika and cavalrymen.

Parichha prostrated before Gajapati and expressed his gratitude and respect for him. The Parichha was Gajapati's nephew, his younger brother Parsuram Harichandan's son Raghudev Narendra Mahapatra.

"Your Highness, you stepped out of Bidanasi Cuttack after so long to come to the south, and we waited eagerly for your presence," asked Raghudev joyfully.

"Let's get into the fort and talk," Gajapati replied shortly. The Gajapati was quite tired and did not want to prolong the conversation.

They covered ten miles in an hour and reached Rajamahendry before time.

Gajapati felt happy at his desired Fort, and his agony vanished. He felt at home inside the Fort. The Gajapati loves the Rajamahendry Fort from his heart as it is the southern stretch of Kalinga or Odisha. He had often halted here since he had recovered it from

Rajamahendry Fort

the clutches of Reddy. Odisha authorities achieved renovation of a critical official site of Odisha Rashtra. The fort area was as big as an elaborate village, and it accommodated many officials, military personnel and temple administration. Refurnishing of the rooms, temple and community completed. The Jagannath Temple inside the Fort had been there since the time of Gangas, even the time of premier Ganga kings, Chodaganga Deva and Narasimha Deva. Formalities of the temple that had gone slack during Reddy's days were ready. The military establishment was nearby, though top military officials resided inside the Fort.

All the Mahapatras and attendants chose their rooms in the Fort. Raghudev Narendra Mahapatra, with some attendants, led Gajapati to his chamber and started looking after him.

"Raghu, Jagannath Himself has given me the

indication to appoint you as Parichha here. See, you are quite capable, for which I got an indicatory sign from the Lord. Isn't it?"

"You alone are the embodiment of the Lord's power. That power can achieve the impossible. The whole world is witness to it today. Only Lord Jagannath has blessed you with that far-sight," Raghudev answered.

A swelling effusion of unrestrained delight from Gajapati's heart kept shining on his face when he realized that very few people throughout Odisha disbelieved his words and ignored the revelatory dream in which Jagannath appeared. My Raghu has perfectly understood me in this, he said to himself. In the figure of Krishna, Jagannath Himself says, "I do, and I get things done, so there is no one else other than me." In such a case, opposing me is opposition to Jagannath. In my life, I have fulfilled my aim of building and strengthening Odisha. But I have been perceived in the public as something precisely the opposite. If this is not my misfortune, what could it be?

A day will come when Odisha people will agree, and the same bunch of garrulous ones will say that Kapilendra Deva has done no wrong in choosing his successor as he had made no mistake in planning any battle. Whatever Jagannath revealed to him in his dream, he bowed to Him in agreement.

His thought got stuck somewhere in that knotted web when Raghudev began speaking, "Your Highness, you look very thoughtful. They say brooding melancholy quickens old age, and persistent morbidity deteriorates health. Your health is deteriorating. Your bright eyes now look lustreless, as if the smile on your face has left you forever. You are living in severe pensiveness. "

Gajapati spoke nothing; he kept looking at Raghu. He thought he lived in a different world. He built such a vast empire, such a substantial giant-size administrative machinery is working for him, and underneath is the enormous military might of Odisha, the soul of which is he, the General of generals. Who forces him to live in a different world, forgetting these glorious achievements? Not only has he withdrawn his mind from that vast panorama, but he has also slunk away from his family and confined himself to his convictions.

Meanwhile, many efficient generals, soldiers, and administrators have looked away in displeasure. Personal relationships in the family, too, have taken a beating. His sons also are silent and non-cooperative. It has ruined the family. Domestic fights in the family are a clear possibility. The earth under his feet is slipping. Perhaps Raghu doesn't know it — no use telling him everything in detail.

"No, nothing like that in my mind, Raghu, you must be watching me. You must be assessing my devotion to Jagannath. I live every moment of my life being guided by Him. The same Lord fixed it, so General Kapilendra became the king. Since Jagannath was so-willed, he spread his controlling influence all over Bharatavarsha. If someone credits all these achievements to Gajapati Kapilendra Deva, he is not a true devotee of Jagannath. Jagannath has helped me in my apprenticeship. Otherwise, neither would I have had such opportunities nor won many battles. Despite all that, I would say that I have been suspected by many family members and colleagues who don't have faith in Jagannath," saying this Gajapati kept mum.

Raghudev could understand that raising the issues of dispute between the two brothers Purushottam and Hamvira Deva, as well as the *Bada Bapa* or great uncle's decision, would cause him immense pain. He thought it better to divert.

Raghudev began, "Really, as folklore goes, the elephant poured the anointing water from the golden pot on your head. It would not have been possible if it had not been for Jagannath's blessings for you. Indeed, you are fortunate to be under the protective arms of His compassion. You may disagree, but people in the know ask me if the living cobra raised its hood above your head while asleep under a tree to foretell in advance that you would be the Gajapati!

"The fact is that, Your Highness, I have framed a lasting answer to it. Calling you lucky is welcome, but for that matter, because you were a poor *Brahmin*, should they cook up such folklore themselves and propagate it? They will ruin our family's reputation. For this reason, I got our Gajapati family's copper plate inscriptions completed. Then I put it in place at Raghudevpur, a newly founded colony about eight koshas (sixteen miles) north of Rajamahendry. And on that plate, I have placed our ancestral achievements down to our times. Is there any way for them to offend our caste and lineage? This metal plate will one day hit the rumour hard and speak about our dynasty in the proper light. The family's name is Odia, and the brothers have taken the titles of Narendra, Harichandan or Routray. Its direct descendant, I, all Parichhas, have done justice to our titles "Raghudev" or "Ganadev Rautray" by our commendable deeds - people don't hesitate to think that such a family alone can be the fitting symbol of *Odia Paika*.

"Let me recite the script on the plate. The General of the Ganga army, Sri Kapileswar Nayak, has a son, Sri Jageswar Nayak. Jageswar was in charge of many elephantry divisions. He had three sons: eldest Balarama, second son Kapilendra, and youngest Parsuram Harichandan. In the space for the inaugurator's name, I am Raghudev Narendra, son of Parshurama Harichandana."

"My son, indeed, you have done a commendable job here. Making a copper plate inscription carrying our credentials and installing it in a village established in your name is the wisest thing ever done. I take that *Kasia-Kapila story* as a joke. Many might believe this popular joke. But when they see this plate, they will turn pale in shame. Your efforts are indeed commendable; you deserve inordinate appreciation.

"It's a matter of great happiness, Raghu. I never paid any attention to it. I don't care for the folklore. Many have asked me about this, but their version I discarded as soon as it came to my knowledge. Compared to them, you are too young for me. My victory over Rajamahendry was twenty years after I acceded to the throne. Kalinga extending from Ganga to Godavari is in my mind. Is Rajamahendry beyond Godavari? How can the Reddy family take forcible possession of the Kalinga boundary for three generations? Last Ganga kings failed to drive them away. Gangaraj *Matta* Bhanudev sat in Simadri for months, retreated to Gudari, and lost the throne. A time came when I, too, gathered the forces of my kingdom and feudatories as far as possible and arrived at Rajamahendry.

"Do you know Raghu what happened after that?" asked Gajapati Kapilendra.

"I have heard a little but don't know much," Raghudev replied.

"If you don't know, listen to who came to our help. Then Birabhadra was the Reddy ruler of Rajamahendry. The Reddy family was in constant trouble on the southern boundary for thirty years or more; first, they occupied Rajamahendry, and soon after that, Simadri and its adjacent regions. That created immense restlessness. *Matta* Bhanudev failed even to get into a compromise with him. I was hopeful that our Rajamahendry campaign would succeed, but alas, we learned that two powerful forces secretly supported Reddy. Vijayanagara ruler Devray had given his ablest General, Malappa Bhodeyar, all the powers to frame strategies and was helping the Reddy.

"Luckily, we withdrew from the undertaking because, just at that time, Jaunpur Mahmud Shah was planning to attack Odisha from the north. We got a fresh chance after two years. The mighty Devray passed away, and his successor, Mallikarjuna, was a weak ruler. Birabhadra Reddy lost all the assistance he received from Vijayanagara. At that time, I sent a vast army under Hamvira Deva 's command. We crushed Birabhadra, and he entirely withdrew from Rajamahendry. However, we had captured Visakhapatnam three years before we annexed Rajamundry and Godavari.

"At the same time, choosing Parichha for the conquered territory became a burden on my head. My eyes fell on my late brother Parsuram's family. And since you were his heir, I sent you here. My trust in you is firming up day by day. If, at these places, we post our blood relations, there is no chance of creating any traitors. A well-organized empire will emerge if we post our blood relations in every feudatory or occupied territory. For about two decades, Rajamahendry has been an integral part of Odisha and is functional as such. Rajamahendry is the most ideal and imitable part of my empire."

"How much are you fond of this Rajamahendry?" Raghudev was curious to know.

Gajapati momentarily mused, saying, "I feel it is an old citadel like Bidanasi Cuttack. Many opine that Rajamahendry is the centre of Telugu culture in our gigantic Odisha. Many centuries ago, the first Telugu poet, Nanaya, translated one-third of Sanskrit Mahabharata into Telugu Mahabharata. He also set an example by forming grammar and script. With him were Tikanna and Yeranna, who together completed Telugu Mahabharata. The standard of this Nanaya is widely discussed in our army because many Telugu-speaking military personnel keep reading Telugu Mahabharata, and that inspires our Odia-speaking soldiers. "

Raghu queried, "Our Odia Mahabharata has been written and dedicated to you. Sarala Das singlehandedly completed Odia Mahabharata in a unique style. I am too stupid a man to tell you anything. You are a writer and a playwright. Who doesn't know that you wrote the Sanskrit play "Parshuram Vijay"? This play has also been enacted before Lord Jagannath on one special occasion in your presence. The depiction of Vishnu, Shiva and Jagannath is there in the play, the story of Parsuram killing Kartviryarjuna and the narrative on queen Chandrabadana. You have deep knowledge of Sanskrit and Odia languages. You have proven that you are a consummate writer. You have also established your knowledge and wisdom as the writer of "Kapila Samhita," showing your great luck and self-esteem in this book. Your deathless couple of lines are there in it:

"VarshanamBharatvarshah | Deshanamutkalasrutah |
Utkalasyasamadeshah | Desanastimaheetale | "

(Of all the lands Bharatavarsha is the greatest, Of all the small regions Utkal is the most renowned, There is no region in this whole world comparable to Utkal)

Utkal, the Excellence of Arts and Crafts

Indeed, my great uncle, your love for the motherland and patriotism are incomparable. We, the people of border areas of Odisha, are enchanted to hear these pieces of news about interior Odisha," Raghudev fixed his eyes on Gajapati.

Gajapati didn't let the discussion stop there. He said, "This Odia Mahabharata was entirely composed by only one man, Siddheswar Parida, whom Goddess Sarala had blessed. I came to know him personally after one caste-based incident crept into Odisha literature. After the completion of Odia Mahabharata, a group of Sanskrit Pandits objected to his writing and underestimated it. But I had gone through the text, which contains pure Odia language that has crystallized through several centuries from spoken words. Never before I imagined that the whole of mountains and rivers would give way to Pandavas, saints and sages of Mahabharata as depicted with originality by Sarala Das. He came for a ceremonial appraisal by Chief Mahapatra Kasinath Mahapatra only two years ago. I learned that he was an armed soldier of the Gajapati military force. He decided among his friends very casually to compose Mahabharata, so he retired from service and, by the grace of Lord Jagannath, held the quill, giving up the sword. SiddheswarParida has proved himself as Sarala Das and has shown what hard labour can do. He has not only translated the theme of the original Mahabharata into pure Odia but also incorporated the background of Odisha, its geography and landmarks like *Kapilash*, *Biraja Kshetra* and *Gandhamardan Mountain* and many other places of Odisha – all of them testify to the identity of Odisha. Indeed, Sarala Das is an example of how a myth-writer can paint the picture of an independent kingdom. The narrow mindedness of Sanskrit writers was exposed when I appreciated the incredible talent of Sarala Das his concept of dedicating an epic in the mother tongue to the people of Odisha in General. The Sanskrit text was definitely beyond comprehension.

"Many outsiders fail to understand that the Odia language has an old and hallowed heritage and that it precisely constitutes the uniqueness of a language. The speech was born out of folklore. There were many scholars in my court. Many of them were repositories of fathomless knowledge of Sanskrit. But they were not so much devoted to the original native language of Odisha. As a responsible son of Odisha, I want the Odia language and culture to have free will from the sway and dominance of Sanskrit.

Popular language alone is suitable for administration. Therefore, I have instructed to form a unique literary platform. If the language and records are in Sanskrit, confine themselves to a handful of educated people. If the language ordinary people speak in the court, and temples are in Odia, it will have far-reaching consequences.

"The writer of *Odia Mahabharata*, Sarala Das, wrote it in the popular *Prakrit* language of Odisha instead of writing in the metrical form of Sanskrit. To write it with native and contemporary characters, he replaced the Himalayas and river Ganga with Kapilas and river Baitarani of Odisha. His depiction of rituals and customs associated with the Jagannath temple, along with Odia militarism and military strategies of

Odia Paika soldiers, showcases his creative genius. The writer has achieved his goal to popularize the epic Mahabharata and prove the uniqueness of the Odia language. The most useful Odia Mahabharata, written by Sudramuni Sarala Das, is a monumental work in the Gajapati kingdom. The issue of Odia Mahabharata is still ongoing. There is no doubt that long into the future, this work will be dazzling one day as Pole Star and will stand as a custodian of our mother tongue."

Gajapati paused for a while.

Just then, Raghudev asked, "You are a landmark in the history of Emperors. You have absorbed not one but many singularities. You have named your kingdom 'Odisha', you have upstaged Kalinga and Utkal names, and the language of the new Odia kingdom is 'Odia'. As you have introduced punitive measures for not using vernacular in official communication, using the Odia medium has gathered momentum quickly. Your patronage of Odia is a glorious chapter in the pages of history as an instance of how everyday language can benefit governance. Kudos for your ideals and your *modus operandi*!

Raghudev continued, "I have never seen your uniqueness in anyone else. You are highly conscious of self-esteem. Today's world knows that you are the strongest of men physically and mentally. Is there any Emperor other than you with a high mind, great spirit, godly intentions, and uniqueness in this world? You rose above politics to name the kingdom suitably. Your talent is so great that you could make Purushottam worshippable for quite a long period, as Sri Jagannath. The same Jagannath has today helped you be the spiritual backbone for Odisha. He alone has been the cosmic force to drive your life. You have laid the foundation stone for golden Odisha. You have covered *Sri Jagannath* with gold. You are the father of *"Gajapatikruta Pagoda"* gold coins. Your coinage will remain an example of Odishan prosperity and self-esteem in future.

You have named Lake Narendra in Purushottam Kshetra after my late father and fourteen jetties after your fourteen nephews, including me. For all times to come, you have introduced the rituals of ChandanYatra."

The Narendra Lake

Gajapati had forgotten that he had accomplished all this over time. Domestic feuds of the past have caused his loss of memory. Today, all that Raghudev has said is the fruit of his devotion to Jagannath, love for the Odia language, and patriotism. Gajapati came out of his reverie. His interest in politics and administration from the military point of view has become disruptive due to family feuds.

Gajapati expressed his will to visit river Godavari as a mark of respect to this famous spiritual site. This river is immensely holy and has its place in all our epics and religious customs. Its purity bears the sanctity of a race – the Odia race is within two great holy waterways of the country – Punyatoya Ganga in the north and Punyatoya pure Godavari in the South—the constant flow in the twin waterways purities Odias' mind to be God-loving. The simple, devoted reason of the Gajapati was searching for a cause of the sanctity of his race.

Raghudev invited the Gajapati to the bank of river Godavari at *Puskara Ghat*, and there was a small worship and offering to *Lord Kotilingeswar*. The offering to the deity satisfied the soul of Kapilendra Deva. He bowed down before God as he usually does. He remembers this temple as he gets immense peace of mind after the visit.

They returned to the Fort in the evening.

Raghudev reminded him. You are to greet

the Odia Paika of Rajamahendry and appreciate their courage. You are an astute military person and never have oversight of military affairs. Since your participation with the army is comprehensive and total, the forces are on eternal vigilance. Our Gajapati forces will always show strength and courage. Had it not been the case, how could this vast Gajapati Empire stand erect in this terrible military environment of rapid changes? In addition, the Gajapati Army is not atrocious. It never allows your name to be soiled. When all over Bharatavarsha, Yavans were out to conquer kingdoms in devious ways, all the subjects hoped that Gajapati would appear as the incarnation of God and rescue them.

Furthermore, they thought that if they remained under Gajapati, Jagannath would bless them and strengthen their faith. They would enjoy the fruits of a fulfilled life. There was uproar in the South, 'Gajapati, take care of religious belief.'

Gajapati, though old, inspected the guard of honour at the Rajamahendry branch of his army. He recommended corrective measures after closely reviewing their elephants, cavalry, and infantry contingents. He addressed them aloud: "Odisha originally extended from Ganga to Godavari, and Rajamahendry was its southern boundary. We will deploy a strong military force, not merely for border security but because the southern boundary has spread farther in our new 'Great Odisha', and so includes

Kondapalli fortress at 120 miles distance from the previous southern boundary; Kondavidu 180 miles away, Karnataka Udayagiri fort 300 miles apart, and Chandragiri fort 400 miles away. This Rajamahendry contingent has a vital role to play in our military needs."

He mused momentarily and then muttered, "Antaranga Mahapatra daily reports to me. He knows that our capital, Cuttack, is at a distance of 280 miles to the northern border of Mandaran, and Chandragiri, on the southern border, is about 840 miles away. Rajamahendri, farther to the South, is 440 miles, and we have occupied another 400 miles down south up to Kanyakumari and Nellore near Arkat. Military institutions are bound to this vast empire's integrity and border security. There is the possibility of sudden invasions by the enemy. Therefore, whatever is necessary for the large territory and complete military strategy of each of our military forces, we must fulfil it in the interest of the kingdom's integrity."

His voice suddenly went up, "So long as the Odia Paika has zeal in his bloodstream, the boundary of Odisha will not yield to any force. No enemy will dare attack Odisha. Our invincibility is a matter of great honour for us. Our dark-skinned elephantry is the backbone of our military and bestows us a feeling of military superiority."

Raghudev kept wondering. Father Senior has not only extended the border of Odisha but also has an account of every inch of Odisha's land distribution at his fingertips. It is impossible to think that a king might entertain such thoughts regarding language, culture and honour in today's world. He cultivated this mindset born out of self-esteem. And he rejoiced at it. When he walked to adorn the throne daily, the herald repeated 'Sri' 108 times before addressing him as *Gajapati-Gaudeshwar-NavakotiKarnata-Kalabargeswar -Biradhibirabara*. He is a staunch supporter of the Odia language. His military planning has always been an example for others. The war drums of the Odisha army are extraordinary; the Gajapati army flag is the symbol and reminder of its pride. It creates the zeal for militarism and the urge for lightning strikes.

At this time, he indicated Antaranga Mahapatra. He hinted to *Purohita* Mahapatra that the time had come for the *Arati* to the deity in Jagannath temple. "Let us move," he said.

The *Purohita* Mahapatra finished the *Arati* ritual offering in the temple. Today, Gajapati is experiencing a lot of restfulness because he could never see his face without the marks of sorrow and shock for at least a fortnight after departure from Cuttack. Today, his mind had changed before Raghudev. Gajapati may take Rajamahendry fortress as his second home.

Purohita Mahapatra said, "Your Majesty, you have installed the idols of Jagannath in all the forts of Odisha along with the arrangement of ritual offerings. These make our migrant Odias and Paikas conscious of the happiness and mental peace they get from worshipping their presiding deity. We are unique and are the subjects of Odisha. The Lord has kept Odia people active through the spiritual fulfilment flowing from Sri Jagannath's inspiration, making them issues of invincible warrior Kapilendra Deva, the emperor of vast and enlarged Huge Odisha, a matter of historical importance. "

"In today's Bharatavarsha, the greatest Hindu king is Gajapati, the ruler of a gigantic Hindu kingdom. In the country, say, Banga, Rajputana, Malwa, Uttara Pradesh or Telangana, Yavans are oppressive, and there are instances of Hindu families migrating to Odisha. For this reason, Cuttack is the third largest city in Bharatavarsha and twelfth in the list of the world's most secure cities during your reign, Your Highness. Gajapati Kapilendra Deva stood as the world's greatest king during his lifetime."

All the statistics *Purohita* Mahapatra presented brought supreme joy to everyone. Everyone was proud of Gajapati's achievements. Odisha is the most secure Hindu kingdom. During the last four decades, when throughout Bharatavarsha Yavans were destroying temples, when no king of the country dared construct a temple, Somavamsi, Gangavamsi, and Suryavamsi Gajapati kings fearlessly went on building and maintaining many shrines. After capturing the Lakhnouti Muslim kingdom as a memorial, Narasimha Deva built Konark of *Arkakshetra*. Before Konark, the construction of the Jagannath Temple at Puri and Lingaraj Temple in Bhubaneswar was over. Temple is the flag of the Hindu religion, the mindset to care for the destructive attitude of Muslims and to disregard the enemy with contempt. It might be the situation elsewhere in India, but can the Muslim power stop the Odia race from building temples? Are we afraid of them exposing their gold ornament-laden appearance?

Gajapati got ready for dinner. Today, Raghudev's truthful words have relieved His Majesty's inner distress. Today, he will have a deep sleep. Even though it has been a fortnight since they departed from Barabati, the Odisha fort on the banks of Krishna is far away. It seems impossible to reach there within a week.

A speck of weariness kept hanging like a strand of dirt in Gajapati's mind. He still said to himself, "It is true that the entire southern region is a vassal kingdom of Odisha. But the most recalcitrant and stubborn is the Vijayanagara kingdom. Its capital, Hampi, has been subjugated and made a vassal kingdom, true, but every moment, it's trying to escape from our dominance. After Devray, his successor, Mallikarjuna, was not a warrior. However, his representative, Saluva Narasimha, frequently intended to capture Chandragiri and Udayagiri regions. Saluva is frantic to snatch away the portion south of river Pinakini, a branch of river Kaveri."

Gajapati said, "Whatever be our strength and efficiency, defence of Kondavidu is our priority.

Ours leaving Rajamahendry tomorrow is inevitable. If we reach Kondapalli soon, we should work on the problem. "

Vespers was about to be over. Country-made torches illuminated Rajamahendry Fort. Gajapati was brooding over something. Raghudev stood silently with his eyes resting on him. He fully knew the contents of his morbid contemplation but couldn't muster the courage to intervene. When the father senior is not opening up to him about his home affairs, how can he ask him? It has been five days since his arrival. Tomorrow, he is going far away. He didn't even make a cursory reference to brother Hamvira Deva. Raghudev had no other option but to keep mum.

Raghudev glanced at Gajapati and saw the constant flow of tears from his sorrowful eyes.

He consoled, "No, please, you shouldn't be worried. You spent your whole life on the battlefield without any remorse. How have you accepted your decision as God's Will in this last part of your life? Who will oppose it? "

He is selfless and stoical. And from his face, none can read his mind. The Lord Himself has ordained in his dream. He must exercise it. Customs for succession aren't comparable with an oracle. To go back on his decision isn't possible on the part of an emperor like him. Let the whole earth be under the deluge; he won't budge.

Raghudev thought it wasn't right to intrude. Will it be proper for him to say in Hamvira Deva 's favour? No, it could not be appropriate. One aspect of the story is that the father was deeply involved with his son for many days and was delighted to enjoy the fruits of victories. The same father has done partiality against the same son!

Another aspect of the story is that the deed must be superhuman if the king should choose him from among many for access to the throne. 'The Emperor who has surrendered himself to Lord Jagannath all his life, why would he disobey now? From this point of view, admiring Hamvira Deva and the love and affection of the whole of the South had for him would be painful for his father,' concluded Raghudev.

The poignant scene of Gajapati Kapilendra Deva's departure is filled with deep emotion and a sense of finality. Raghudev, overwhelmed by the situation, struggled to find words to comfort or advise his great uncle, recognising that sometimes silence is the best response to life's challenges. Gajapati, in his wisdom, offered profound reflection on the unpredictability of life and the need to accept God's will, even when faced with circumstances beyond our control. As Gajapati prepared to leave, the touching interaction between him and Raghudev revealed the depth of their relationship. Raghudev accompanied him for a significant part of the journey, symbolising their bond and the deep respect Raghudev held for his great uncle. Gajapati's departure with folded hands was a departure from tradition, leaving Raghudev puzzled and wondering about its significance.

The scene is laden with emotion and foreshadows the uncertainties of life. It captures the essence of Gajapati Kapilendra Deva's final journey and the complex emotions experienced by those who witnessed the departure.

A relaxing photo of Gajapati

Gajapati Fort on Koleru Lake

In the military camp where Gajapati rested for the next night, he couldn't sleep well despite all the comforts. He recalled how much he felt at home during the five-day sojourn with Raghudev. At the time of departure, Raghudev's touching his feet made him so tender that he couldn't hold his tears. Taking leave from Raghudev with folded hands was not a predetermined act. He wondered if he would meet Raghudev again. He is still determining if he will return and see Raghudev on his way back.

Antaranga Mahapatra told Gajapati that day, "Since we are rushing, do you feel any pain in the body or head? If you so desire, we can slow down. This way, there will be time, only a day or half a day more.

Gajapati thought a little and said, "Antaranga, how long have you been with me? Thirty years have passed since the second year of my accession, and now you ask me if I have any physical pain or headache.

Has my race against time ever deterred me? How often didn't Jaunpur Nawab force us to increase our pace manifold?

"At one time, if we put our army in fighting array before Rajamahendry Birabhadra Reddy and at some other time, our spy came running to the battlefield with the news of Jaunpur forces marching towards Odisha. For this, when we were fighting with Bahamani Bidar, we rushed to the north without delay. Then why should our fast pace pain our limbs?"

It is three days since Gajapati's royal party left Rajamahendry Fort. They aimed to reach the island fortress and rest in that new environment for a day. Their tour began in the lunar month of Margasira. It was harvest time everywhere. Farmers crowded the paddy fields harvesting the crop. After the dewy season was gone, Nature's greenery and the hints of winter set aliveness in every heart in myriad hues. In tune with Nature's smile, fruits and flowers in the green bosom of the forests came up to show unprecedented harmony—the signs of joy and sweet feelings inundated with these manifestations on the earth. Gajapati's horse-drawn coach assumed more incredible speed, and the six Mahapatras rode behind on horseback. Besides, innumerable Odia intelligence officials and soldiers were busy with their duties. The Gajapati could see the beauty of Nature, but he had lost his aesthetic sense of enjoying it. His military attitude debarred him, receiving pleasure from the scenic beauty of the picturesque plain land they were moving through.

In the afternoon of the fourth day, they were on the bank of Koleru Lake. This lake was the second one they were confronting; it was another vast one after traversing so far and passing through the Chilika Lake, which remained almost ten days of travel distance. Koleru is smaller than Chilika and less deep. The Koleru Lake is a vast water body full of soft water. The Gajapati fortress is an island-like place in the Eastern part of this lake. Lake water surrounds it, some fifty-two miles from the Rajamahendry border. It is a secure fort some seventy miles from the traditional south edge of Odisha, looking like a remote satellite of Odia Paikas.

The Fort Authority welcomed Gajapati on arrival as per naval protocol. He enjoyed appropriate royal honour and hospitality. Besides hundreds of housekeeping employees in this Fort, a military contingent was always ready for emergencies. VijayaBahuda, or Vijayawada, was only 40 miles from here, and Elluru is its nearby city.

After continuously riding on horseback for four days, Gajapati could reach Koleru Fort. Soon, it was evening. The lake water around reflected the dazzling rays of the setting sun only to remind Gajapati of bloodbaths in battles. The loud cries of migratory birds in the month of Margasira and the usual commotion on the earth have painted the picture of many actions in his mind. For the king who had spent most of his life on the battlefield, the music of all that noise and voice appeared like the war cry of war drums.

Despite sorrow clouding his heart, he proudly considered this Gajapati Fort at Koleru as a pillar of daredevilry. True, he has not built this Fort. He doesn't know who made it centuries ago, some Gangaraj or someone much before him. But he knew this secret when he was an efficient General of Odia Paika regiment. This secret Gajapati Fort functioned even though there were enemies all around! You know how Rajamahendry's military post secretly managed it.

After a little while, the Superintendent of Fort Ratnakar Gumanasingh got permission for an audience. Following a brief discussion, he informed Gajapati that all the Mahapatras and inmates were waiting for him in the nearby temple for a ritual evening offering, the aarati. Instantly, Gajapati joined the rituals in the temple. Gajapati looked at Jagannath's face. His joyful thoughts swelled at the musical rhythm of the collective prayer and lifted him to the Puri Jagannath temple at Puri. He felt blessed to see Jagannath. But he asked the Lord, "Lord, this 'Rauta' was created by you, led by your indications. Why is he left to be offended like that? Can he not ascertain? Please teach me where I lack."

He continued looking at Lord Jagannath for a long time. He stood, saying nothing. All the people of the Fort finished worshipping. All of them were waiting for Gajapati to come out of his prayerfulness, with his eyes flooding with tears. Finally, Gajapati looked at them.

In a trembling voice, he said, "I had also renovated Gajapati Fort. After constructing the Jagannath Temple here, I created opportunities to perform rituals for the Lord in the same pattern as in Puri. I feel now that Jagannath is in manifestation here."

Gajapati said, "It's late from my end. Let's assemble in the meeting hall for a while before dinner. "The superintendent arranged a meeting. Gajapati sat in a chair, and other officials with Mahapatras sat on palm-leaf mats. Gajapati said, "The location of this Fort in a hideout, I can't figure out who can convey to us its true history of Koleru Gajapati Water Castle with a definite aim to ward off enemy's easy approach. The secret behind such a strategic military spot crops up in my mind whenever I come here, but it hasn't been possible till today due to the time factor. I have some direct knowledge about its military importance. Once, we went from this Fort with forces at night, reached Devarakonda on a surprise visit, befooled Bahamani and defeated his army with a severe stroke. From then onwards, our route to Telangana opened up. I forgot many things today. The momentous heritage of this Fort I can't remember in detail. Yet our superintendent or *Sandhibigraha* can enlighten us with all the details. We are waiting; whoever knows it may give us the details."

The Fort Superintendent stood up and begged for permission to speak. Gajapati said, "Since I have asked for it, you or *Sandhibigraha* can proceed with the details. If anyone else knows something more, may volunteer to add."

Gumanasingh said, "What we, the inmates of this Fort, know is that some Odia king built it long ago, maybe three or more centuries. It's unclear who built it and why, but the possible reasons could be military, security, and intelligence. It is so old that powerful Narasimha Deva, two hundred years back, also knew its presence. Possibly before Yavan forces marched into the South, they built a secret strategy on the island at the lake's centre. As Lord Narasimha often liked the term 'Gajapati', most possibly he had named so."

Sandhibigraha Mahapatra began, "The fact is that when we call it Gajapati Fort, it means the name came after Narasimha Deva. The proof that he alone of the Ganga dynasty had assumed the title 'Gajapati' is found on inscriptions on Kapilash Mountain, where Narasimha Deva had inscribed 'Gajapati'. He was invading Muslim kingdoms of Bengal in the north; it seems that he intended to enhance the area of Kalinga Dandapata beyond Rajamahendry. For this reason, he might have built this Fort."

Sandhibigraha continued, "Another myth is there in villages beside Koleru Lake. Mahamadin from the enemy stayed at Chigurukota on the bank of the lake and got a hint that a secret fort of the Kalinga King existed somewhere nearby. This Fort is in the middle of the lake, which is the deepest; it is not easy to reach it. Mahamadin decided to arrange for a group of many locals to attack the Fort. He applied his mind and decided that they would dig a channel to drain out water so that a large number of soldiers could reach the Fort without difficulty. One day, when they started digging from the Uputeru end, the work was so fast-paced that the lake would be empty by morning to make forces' entry easy. And by sunrise, Gajapati Fort would be under the enemy's control.

"But the daughter of Gajapati fort-in-charge heard this, and she lay across the hole all night blocking the flow and thus didn't let the water flow out. The General looking for his daughter finally was an eyewitness to her night-long ceaseless labour at the water hole. He saw that she alone saved the Fort from the enemy's hands. Her attempt foiled the enemy's conspiracy and could rescue the Fort at the cost of her own life. All the inhabitants of Koleru Lake were already the Gajapati's supporters; they now feel proud of the adventurous work done by the womenfolk of the region.

The story of Pedentilama's courageous act in saving the Fort and her ultimate sacrifice deeply moved the audience. He selfless devotion and bravery touched their hearts, and many were brought to tears by her example. Gajapati Kapilendra Deva, too, was profoundly affected by the story and the emotions it evoked.

As Sandhibigraha shared the story and mentioned the Pedentilama Tample near koletikota, Gajapati expressed his admiration for the deep-seated sentiments of the Jagannath Cult that had a profound influence on Odia society. He recognised how the ideals and character of Lord Jagannath had shaped the values and conscience of the people, instilling in them a sense of familial and social responsibility, as well as a strong foundation in humanism.

This moment reflected the power of storytelling and the impact of historical and mytological narratives in shaping the cultural and ethnical values of a society. It also showcased the empathetic and reflective nature of Gajapati Kapilendra Deva, who found inspiration in the stories of courage and sacrifice.

Gajapati turned his face to another direction and said, "We shall certainly visit tomorrow the shrine, the great Pedentilama, our highly revered goddess and rest there. But today, her sacrifice, holy men and Generals and soldiers who risked their lives on the battlefield, who have dedicated their energy and time as and when needed for Odisha Kingdom - all of them are coming to my mind as heroes who deserve our gratitude. I want to admire their greatness one by one personally.

"Countless soldiers, Generals, Bahinipatis and Chapatis, elephants, and horses have snatched victory from the enemy, sacrificing their lives. Undoubtedly, these lives must be in circumstances resembling

Pedentilama's. No one can give a complete account of those spies and security forces that might have laid down their lives for us and that no one knows. They are worthy of our salutation forever.

"Many brave souls have actively contributed to the expansion of the Gajapati Empire. Many are still alive and have established themselves in their native areas. I welcome them on behalf of Odisha Rastra and

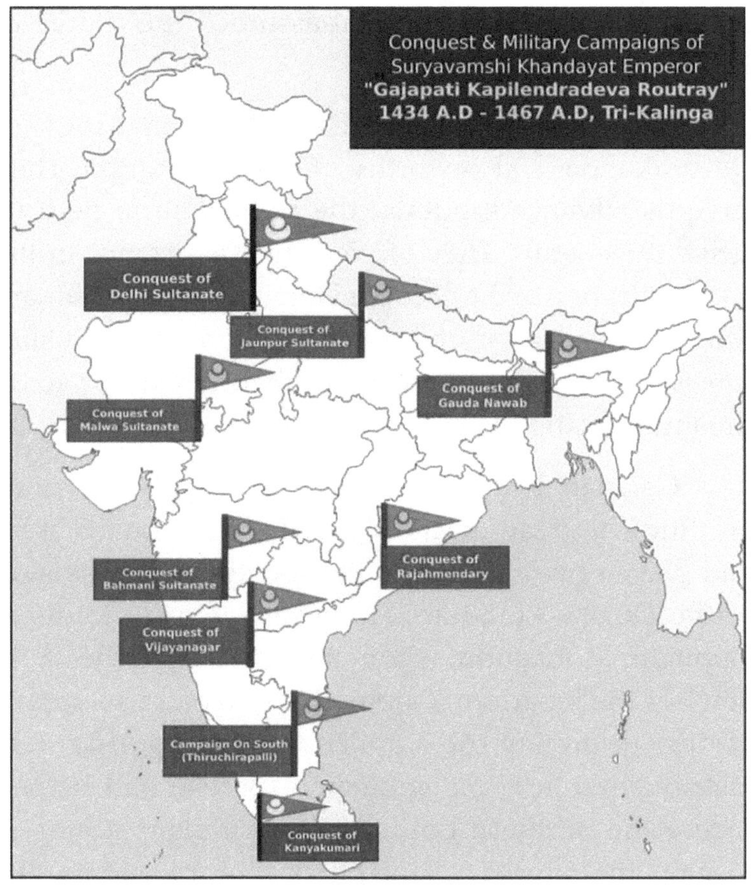

Gajapati Kapilendra's Bharata Vijaya

thank them. Considering their contributions, they were all helpful at critical times. And that is good fortune for Odisha.

"Two leading personalities outside Odisha have amply supported our attempts to dominate in the South. Tuma Bhopal of Telangana once captured Udayagiri from Saluva Narasimha six years ago as the non-Odia General of the Gajapati Squad. For this reason, his son Basab Bhupal assumed the charge of Udayagiri as Parichha.

"The Hindu Velama chief Madaya Linga of Devarakonda is also worthy of our admiration. They gave us advance inputs at the right time to help us strike the enemy. They offered their assistance in the administration of the occupied territory. The Bahamani Empire collapsed in the twinkling of an eye. Muslim forces got such a sound beating that they never again dreamt of going to war against us."

Gajapati Kapilendra Deva expressed his deep gratitude and admiration for the individuals who had played pivotal roles in the success and expansion o fthe Odisha kingdom. He began praising Minister Gopinath Mohapatra, whom he describes as the "Pole Star" of the kingdom. Gopinath Mohapatra's support at the beginning of Kapilendra Deva's rule was instrumental, and his strategic expertise had helped secure the northern border and formulate strategies to gain the support of neighbouring kingdoms like Jaunapur, Delhi and Malwa.

The Trinity

The Gauda kingdom in Banga had also been conquered under Kapilendra Deva's rule, with Narendra Mahapatra taking charge of Parichha. Gajapati Kapilendra Deva acknowledged the contributions of his famil members, including his grandson Kumar Dakshineswar Mahapatra, who managed thestrategic Fort of Kondapalli. He also mentioned his nephew, Raghudev Narendra Mahapatra, who served as Parichha of Rajamahendry, and his son Hamvira Deva Mahapatra, who had played a crucial role as the invincible General of Odisha, leading the kingdom to greater glory and dignity.

But just then, Antaranga Mahapatra thought he must speak something. He wondered how Gajapati could admire his good son Hamvira Dev so much. Certainly, Gajapati has changed today. But is there truth in it? He can juggle like a magician. Gossip among the public also was full of the same matter. If Lord Jagannath truly changes his insistence on the succession issue, a conjurer will juggle his activities. From that, it is clear if he is the Lord's devotee or an illusionist. Gajapati has directed me to set out for Kondapalli soon. The movement of troops to the South had been fifteen days since. Kondavidu's southern regions needed immediate attention. We occupied it two years ago. Simply occupying a territory isn't enough; administrative steps should be appreciated by one and all.

Kondavidu Fort

Visit to the Pedentilama temple on the way has been over. Gajapati could realize how dedicated souls like the deity there could serve Odisha, though not her motherland. He was moved with piety and bowed before such a deity.

Now, the coaches were ready. Gajapati and all the Mahapatras started towards the Kondapalli fortress.

Hampi, Capital of Vijayanagara

Fort Kondapalli

Gajapati Fortress of Koleru Lake always held immense hopes in Kapilendra Deva's mind. Such capability alone was the symbol of the invincibility of the Odia race. Enemies had invaded the Odisha region so many times. Enemies have attacked from all sides. But a handful of Kalinga kings got their army ready to fight them back, defeat them and enlarge their territory. About two centuries of occupation of the Gajapati fortress at Kolleru by the Odia army suggests the battle-ready status of Odia Paikas.

Not that Gajapati Kapilendra Deva was coming to Kondapalli for the first time. He had camped here many times. He knew that the honour he got there was mere lip service. He is also the father of a brave son like Hamvira Deva. This feeling hurt his conscience. Previously, he ignored this feeling, but family bitterness asked him to analyze whether Hamvira Deva conquered Kondavidu alone profoundly. Had this Kapilendra not ordered, had he not sent his vast army with him, could the prince alone have won this southern region ruled by Vijayanagara?

Gajapati on Horseback

Gajapati reached Kondapalli the next noon. Kondapalli Parichha Kapileswar Mahapatra was waiting not far off. People there also called him Dakshineswar Mahapatra. He is Hamvira Deva's son and Kapilendra Deva's grandson. Even though Gajapati was his grandpa, Dakshineswar didn't like to take it only as a family affair. Instead, he received him according to royal protocol.

Dakshineswar prostrated before Grandpa. He thanked his grandfather for arriving at Kondapalli in his hour of need. He enquired about the likely weariness from lengthy travel. The grandson wanted to delight him as much as possible. Then he led him to the Gajapati's Chamber and requested him to rest a while. Dakshineswar was putting up in the Parichha Chamber close to the Gajapati Chamber.

Dakshineswar Kumar grinned and said, "Grandpa, why do not you look like my grandpa at Barabati and like an all-conquering hero here at Kondapalli? Why does such a notion come to me?"

He was only twenty-four and a young man from the Gajapati family. Hamvira Deva's son had a handsome figure, smiling face, and snow-white body; he is Dakshineswar, accomplished in all arts. Many called him Kapileswar after his grandfather's name on dynasty considerations. He sat beside Grandpapa and listened to his narration about battles. He watched a play 'Parsurama Vijay' written by his grandfather, and one day asked him," Grandpapa, you are a great combatant. You saw in the Puranas that Parshurama is an astute warrior. You wrote a play on him. Bravery is your viewpoint. Today, my grandfather is the most powerful commander of war on earth. You are today's Parshurama. Parshurama cleansed the world of the warring Kshatriya caste, eliminating them to the last man. But my grandfather has freed our country, Bharatavarsha, from Yavan infiltrators."

Dakshineswar was thinking, "Well, agreed that today grandfather is eighty. Since my boyhood, I've been finding Grandpa enjoying a sound physique and the figure of a highly optimistic man. Nothing in this world is impossible for him. He puts his head into every work and comes out with flying colours. Something strange, he pokes his nose in impossible jobs and, to the utter surprise, comes out successful."

One day, I asked him, "Grandpa, who do you love the most?"

Grandpa replied, "I love all those who love themselves and their own country, those who learn swordsmanship and come forward to fight for their motherland. I castigate sluggish, aimless and haphazard people."

"Indeed, Grandpa, you had engaged several teachers to teach me in the Odia language. At the same time, you had engaged a group of trainers to teach me how to defend myself from a powerful enemy, fight, hold swords and lances, and ride on horseback. You have so much affection for me; I could feel it. I remember you have a pet tusker in the dip-wad close to our Barabati Castle. But you also got one small baby tusker for me, and that faithful one was named Kalia. Kalia loved me so much and had an instinct of friendship with me. I have spent more than ten years with him. Kalia wept when he did not see me for a few days. Even today, he is at home and cries out when he casually sees me when I visit the Barabati Castle. You are so affectionate, Grandpa; I pour my utmost regards to you. You were so concerned when my studies and military training ended that you made me Parichha of Chandragiri."

Dakshineswar went on speaking appreciatively. He knew his grandfather was a man of pleasant disposition.

Kapilendra Deva always called him lovingly "Trutiya", which means a third down the family tree. "The third down the line" means his grandson, "second" means Kapilendra, and "first" means Kapilendra's grandfather. All these three have the same name, 'Kapil or Kapileswar'". The progressive Paika caste of Paikamala Khordha has a custom of naming their children. Gajapati's musings also ran parallel to Dakshineswar's, and his thoughts rolled ceaselessly like the current of a perennial streamlet. This Kapilendu was worming with a lofty, proud pace to meet Grandpa, proving to be eminent in Gajapati's family line. He wanted to hear stories of the last battle. What exciting things were there in the newly conquered kingdom? Where did its royal couple go? The child he was, he had a strong urge to ask whatever questions came to him.

One day, an uncomfortable question slipped loose, "Grandpa, when I shall grow up into a man, shall I wear your Gajapati's crown?"

Today, the same question was agitating him. The flow of his thoughts suddenly got arrested.

Verily true! Even though his "Trutiya" in the present situation is the eldest child of one Gajapati generation, he hasn't had the luck to get crowned. Gajapati couldn't think further. Unable to unwind the knotted yarn of regrets, he prayed to Jagannath, losing himself in his thoughts. He did not get the crown by inheritance; the Lord gave it to him. If the Lord so wishes, "Trutiya" too can get it. He has that much faith and confidence in Him.

He is trying to remember how Gajapati decided to anoint an unripe boy as Parichha. He never intended to appoint distant relations or unknown persons as Parichha of captured territories. And he has experienced the importance of this step. Following his accession, many Parichhas and feudatories paid no heed to the Odisha royal treasury. Hence, in matters of administration, Gajapati has posted only his blood relations.

When we captured Chandragiri from Vijayanagara, Dakshineswar was by then twenty-four. He had mastered studies and martial arts. So, he was given the responsibilities of these areas as Parichha. Gradually, we occupied many feudatories, and all of them were under this newly appointed Parichha. Kondapalli, Adanki, Bhinukonda, Padavidu, Tiruvaruru, Sabhadi, Bhaludulampatu, Tiruchirapalli and many others came under him.

Gajapati, in great delight, affectionately addressed this young Parichha as "Trutiya" and asked, "Any problems in your land?"

Dakshineswar replied, "Although there have been no untoward incidents, Saluva Narasimha's forces have become active on Pinakini Bank south of the Kaveri River in the Udayagiri region. And due to the irresponsibility of our army, Vijayanagara has infiltrated some areas."

Gajapati said, *"Sandhibigraha* Mahapatra, Calculate how many cavalrymen are available in nearby camps and the number of soldiers posted there. We must take a decision."

In the meantime, old Kondavidu Parichha Ganadev Rautray arrived.

Fort Kondavidu has been under the rule of Odisha since its occupation fourteen years ago. Its location on the common border of Odisha and Vijayanagara made it extremely sensitive. Before this, it had been a vassal kingdom of Vijayanagara since Reddy's rule. Therefore, Vijayanagara's constant greed for it was a distinct possibility. Gajapati appointed his blood relations or close minions in this important Fort. He did an intensive search and finally chose his nearest connection, Ganadev. Ganadev Rautray has been Parichha since then. Ganadev was an experienced administrator. He has made outstanding contributions to the victorious battles of Odisha.

Ganadev has come to seek advice from Gajapati regarding some minor issues. Luckily, both Gajapati and Dakshineswar Kumar were present. These three could together discuss Vijayanagara borders. They discussed and decided on the contemporary military situation.

Ganadev prostrated before Gajapati to pay his respects. Gajapati looked at him steadily from head to toe. The presence of an intimate Parichha and valiant

General after so long a time delighted him profusely. Gajapati spoke, his voice choking, "Ganadev, you were just a Parichha then and yet could make Reddy of Kondavidu lick the dust twelve years ago!"

Bahamani Battle

A tiny ripple of memory glistened in his mind. Ganadev was only his distant relation. His grandfather's name was Chandradev, and his father was Gruhadev. He had, in his lifetime, defeated two Turkish Generals. He had been conferred the title of Rautray by Gajapati for achieving that unprecedented glory.

After a while, Gajapati got into informal conversations on some urgent matters with the two Parichhas.

Many more military officials were waiting to meet Gajapati. The ruling of Gajapati's order was necessary for a few problems found in the newly conquered territories. Gajapati directed *Sandhibigraha*

Mahapatras, accompanying him to look into all those matters.

Some incidents undoubtedly have caused a commotion in the office of Kondapalli, the southern centre of Odisha administration. Odisha forces have occupied large Telangana tracts in the last four years. Still, Vijayanagara has been trying to push the Gajapati army from the Pinakini river bank northward.

The Parichha informed Gajapati that Vijayanagara ruler Saluva Narasimha put in much effort and drove out our Odisha army further north. Of course, it needs to establish Vijayanagara's success conclusively. Vijayanagara can't withstand our onslaughts. But because of the inaction of some frontier commanders, Vijayanagara was able to penetrate our territory gradually and forced our men to retreat.

Gajapati was thoughtful. His campaigns were successful, and Odisha's boundary extended threefold. Except for Kalinga Sagar on the east coast, the northern borders of Banga and Bihar have always been alarming—problems multiplied after Odisha occupied the north and South parts of the kingdom. As a matter of security, sufficient forces are necessary for the day. Gajapati realized, proportionate to the new territory, that the spread of the army was inadequate. It was easy to conquer a large bulk of kingdoms due to the vigorous, robust and imposing elephant force. Military and population were working through lengthy supply lines.

"It is not impossible", thought Gajapati, "Odisha has immeasurable human and material resources. We can recruit large cavalry and infantry and increase our sufficient elephant forces.

Comparatively, Vijayanagara has the sea on two sides, unlike Odisha, which has it on one side only. So, it is the urgency of the hour that Gajapati has to muster a lot of force for solid resistance against the enemy. Similarly, Bahamani is another hostile kingdom that doesn't have a long common boundary with Odisha. Apart from the edges of these two kingdoms, Odisha has to be wary of Jaunpur Nawab in the north. If we enhance the Paika army manifold, the captured territories will not only slip out, but the enemy will march into the Odisha border just as well."

Kapilendra Deva's experience of Jaunpur in his tenure was very complex. Jaunpur was a Muslim kingdom six hundred miles from the capital city of Cuttack. It had deployed spies to track the activities of Gajapati forces. Of course, Odisha, Bahamani, and Vijayanagara are not second to each other in the intelligence input collection. But Jaunpur eyes Odisha even though it's not its neighbour. When Odisha forces are engaged in essential battles in the South, Jaunpur threatens to invade Odisha like someone lying in wait to trap and rob. Repeatedly, Kapilendra Deva himself, with all his military wings, had to withdraw from battlefields in the South and rush across eight hundred miles to check Jaunpur. A long border of a ruling kingdom has such deadly and sinister consequences.

Amid all these thoughts, Gajapati took a break for a while. This visit to Kondapalli was his second time. He heard it was a fully secured fort and was the central administrative unit in the far South. Only three years since it came under Odisha's rule, its location is favourable for military movement. From here, can army detachments be sent to far-flung Forts as and when urgency arises?

A golden opportunity three years ago he saw in his mind's eye. It was an incident that happened in *Kapilabda* 28 (1463 AD). The Odisha elephant divisions could capture parts of the Tamil kingdom up to the banks of the Kaveri River. After that, Dakshineswar Mahapatra was appointed Parichha of the newly acquired territory. The Odia army had its eyes fixed on Bidar, the capital city of the kingdom captured by a Bahamani Muslim ruler.

Property feuds, like the fable of the monkey and two cats, came out in Telangana the same year. "When two people fight, it's always the third person who gets the benefit". Two brothers, Ambar Ray and Mangal Ray, had a cat's quarrel, hankering after the throne. Ambar sought Kapilendra Deva's help. Mangal took shelter under Bahamani. There was a treaty on this matter between Odisha and Bahamani. Ambar Ray surrendered the Kondapalli fortress to Kapilendra Deva to earn his trust. Odia soldiers continued their formidable attack on Bahamani. Ten thousand foot soldiers and eight thousand cavalrymen fought in the battle. Gajapati Army massacred many Bahamani soldiers. Ambar Ray was acknowledged as the winner and remained Odisha's vassal.

Yet Kapilendra couldn't get Kondapalli immediately. The queen of the fortress resisted. Her name was Chandrabala, and she was a brave woman. After further fighting, many were felled, and ultimately, we imprisoned her. The Odia flag fluttered on Kondapalli. Kapilendra Deva had come to this Kondapalli once earlier. Reaching for the second time, he found a lot of changes there. We arranged a grand reception in the fortress for the Odia military forces. This Fort catered to the urgent needs of the various occupied territories.

Odia soldiers are very much pious. When they are away from their native land, they habitually show spirituality and devotion to Jagannath. This religious feeling was not simply for courage, bravery and firmness. Instead, it helped them to accept any place as their native soil. Every fortress had a Jagannath temple with provisions for worshipping the deity. But in some forts, worship of existing Gods was allowed to continue.

Kondavidu Fort came under the rule of Odisha fourteen years ago, in *Kapilabda* 18. By then, Odia soldiers had installed Lord Jagannath there and worshipped Him. Balagopal has been installed and honoured in Udayagiri Fort for the last three years. When Lord Jagannath or any of his images are associated with Odia militarism, the mental strength of Paikas soars up, and they experience sociability and humanism. An idea is born in their minds that Jagannath, too, always keeps standing beside them on the battlefield.

Dakshineswar didn't know how to read his grandpa's mind, but he could surmise from the expression that he was still roaming in his past. He spoke, "Grandpa, why are you thoughtful so much?"

Gajapati came out of his reverie and said, "Nothing. I was thinking of the deities in our forts. Do you know how much physical and mental balance these deities ensured for temple servitors, soldiers guarding the deity and residents of the forts? Soldiers feel an innate helplessness when there is no deity in a temple. Jagannath alone is the mental support for these soldiers who are always away from home and leading a life full of danger."

Dakshineswar then said, "You are right, Grandpa. We Odias live with much devotion; Jagannath alone is our ideal. We firmly believe that Lord Jagannath will assist us in times of woe because we have revered Him as our ideal, so much so that Jagannath helps us win any fortress.

Jagannath, in the native places of devotees, is protecting them there. He is all-seeing and all-powerful. The consciousness and thoughts of His cosmic life influence Odia's thinking process. When Odia leaves his home, he takes all his decisions as if Jagannath is taking it for him.

Gajapati felt relaxed during these discussions with his grandson. He felt homely here at Kondapalli. Discussion of Lord Jagannath washed away much of his agony. He felt assured that the great Gajapati Army behind him could protect his kingdom, Lord Jagannath's kingdom.

An emotional Gajapati gave a hug to his grandson, holding him in his arms with natural affection before concluding the conversation.

Gajapati

The Tragic Fall

From the day Kondapalli came into Odisha's hands, military and administrative offices are working fine. But unless the king did something highly religious for Jagannath, it would not be treated by the people of Odisha as a real victory. And many officials have realized it. To this end, of course, one Jagannath temple has been built, and a particular type of *Neem* wood, known as *Daru Brahma*, has been brought, the idol made. More icons are in the making.

Gajapati went to the temple and was delighted to notice the progress. The question agitating him was that he could not certainly feel when the temple construction was over and Jagannath installed.

Gajapati Kapilendra Deva himself was stunned. He is the man who thought his strength was perennial. The legend goes that he prayed and wrote a letter to God Indra to cause heavy showers! All the subjects evaluated his ability to gauge enemy strength and his presence of mind as extraordinary. Then what has happened to such a person's mind that he failed to guess anything about the future?

Gajapati was disturbed. He never expected to be a victim of such forgetfulness and would be stone-blind to the future. Then Gajapati began to fear that it was the vengeful act of some superhuman malevolent force. He went on contemplating this problem repeatedly. Indeed, his mind suddenly has gone blank. He has already announced that he will not return to Odisha. He left Odisha sulking before Jagannath. But now, what is all this happening?

Where has his memory gone? Is it true that he has lost his memory due to family disputes? During the last five years, he had left home only for short spells to travel to distant borders. He was giving all responsibilities to Hamvira Dev in the previous fifteen years. But from the time he got that divine revelation in his dream, "Purushottam born to Parvati Devi will ascend the throne by succession." He was no longer willing to give any responsible work to Hamvira Dev.

Still, he had retained his power to think. He had rushed to the bank of Krishna River to fulfil the vow that he wouldn't part with an inch of the fortress territory he had acquired. Of course, he doubted family quarrels had forced many Generals, *Bahinipatis* and *Champatis*, to be indifferent and opposed to him. It had adversely affected Mandaran and many other southern forts. Who could be behind all that? Gajapati knew he wasn't directly involved in it. Could it be the outcome of Hamvira Deva's influence? Is there a bitter feeling between the father and his formidable son, deprived of the title to the throne? No, surely not. The reason could be the father's step-motherly attitude. This matter, too, was well-known to Gajapati. His doubts were getting thicker. Who else could have created such anarchy?

Gajapati himself is the eyewitness to the fact that uncertainty and indiscipline have been noticed on the northern and southern borders since the news of family bickering spilt out. The single-mindedness and integrity of Odia soldiers were diluted in strength and quality. The truly Odisha army is very much dutiful. But the enemy is so inclined to immorality that they ensnare opposite army officers, including generals and group commanders, with bribes and win battles without difficulty. I'm lucky that such corruption has not seeped into the Paika army. If some army man got such a possibility to accept bribes, he must have withdrawn from it, recalling Gajapati's spotless personality. However, it is crystal clear that this immorality will infect Odia soldiers. The injustice done by the Gajapati royal family will stand before him as the cause of such anarchy. In future, even within his knowledge, army commanders, conveniently bribed, will feign defeat by the enemy. The downfall of Odisha will begin from that day.

Gajapati was terrified at such thoughts he never entertained before. He never put himself in Hamvira

Deva 's position, never read his mind. The Gajapati never asked Hamvira Deva about this issue. So, it's still being determined whether he would accept Jagannath's dream revelation.

Is there Hamvira Deva 's hand behind whatever was happening or would happen in Chandragiri and Udayagiri? There was an attempt to re-capture the tract seized in the past by Vijayanagara. Gajapati needs to be made aware. Hamvira Deva might have some relationship with Bahamani but not with Vijayanagara. Still, Hamvira Deva's incoherent behaviour, the loud silence and the resignation of Odisha army officers - can it all happen without someone's instigation? The thing that never happened in his entire lifetime, how could it happen now?

All such brooding, at last, began to break his firmness. His anxiety shot up. He couldn't sleep out of distress. On the strength of his giant-sized army's perfect single-mindedness, he used to live hundreds of miles away from his citadel. If that army were not convenient to him for some reason, it would not be accessible on his part.

One morning, he called *Sandhibigraha* Mahapatra and said, "I had a nightmare last night. When our Odia Paikas were preparing valiantly to occupy Chandragiri and Udayagiri, Saluva Narasimha's forces turned into monsters. Our soldiers went into hiding out of fright, keeping themselves out of sight."

Gajapati said, mumbled something indistinctly, but *Sandhibigraha* thought that Gajapati had lost his reason. Why is it that today he has sunk in illusions although such derangement never occurred before? Is it due to his hunger for more territory or fear of Hamvira Dev? It could be for something else. Fear and greed cause behavioural changes in ripe old age.

Now, for no compulsive reasons, Gajapati is spreading the message that Odia forces conquered all of Bharatavarsha on their own, and his eldest son Hamvira Dev had no contribution to this; he is not qualified to be the Gajapati of Odisha, Lord Jagannath alone always chooses the successor. He then spoke, "He only made me Gajapati. And He will choose my successor that way. "

Sandhibigraha had no guts to say anything. He had no alternative but to push it to the back of his mind. He was amazed to see such a great emperor, an organizer of a gigantic military force, the brave warrior king in his state of senility. He was an ardent follower of truth and rationalism lifelong. He was the greatest devotee of Jagannath. Who will dare speak to him if he can't know black from white?

Gajapati often sat with his Mahapatras and spoke aloud to reassure them, "Can any kingdom other than ours collect countless Paika soldiers and so many elephants and horses to grab even an inch of our land? It is just impossible. Our Paika soldiers are on guard at Mandaran Fort beside the river Ganga to the southern point at Chandragiri, Udayagiri and Vijayanagara. Who has the guts to confront us?"

Udayagiri Fort

All the Mahapatras heard everything but remained silent. Gajapati got self-satisfaction, although they spoke incoherently. "We are already neck-deep in slush. It's not suitable to wax in pride. Mandaran, too, stands solid as before.

Moreover, Vijayanagara is raising its head. Gajapati's family quarrels have spread everywhere, in and outside the kingdom. Gajapati must be suspecting Hamvira Dev has left Odisha's army and joined the enemy camp. Seen from another point of view, defeated and discontented vassal kingdoms must be dreaming that they have become enormously influential after giving shelter to Hamvira Dev."

The stay at Kondapalli has already been a week. Every day, Gajapati keeps harping on the revelation in dreams. Each morning, one of the two *Purohita* Mahapatras submits to him the details of rituals in the Puri temple and Jagannath's dress and ornaments. Gajapati feels elated. He soothes himself and recalls what *Leela* of Jagannath must be going on at Puri."

"The pot is the measure of water in it; blessings of God rest on the intensity of devotion to him. We are not at Puri, but Jagannath is in our hearts happily paving the way for us to truth," he would say.

Gajapati has been asking the *Purohita* Mahapatra so many times. He also repeats here at Kondapalli fortress, "Have you Mahapatra experienced the Lord directly?"

Purohita Mahapatra replied briefly, "Yes, Your Majesty, I guess He is looking at me always with his round eyes."

"There have been moments in my life when I get a hint of His miracles, and when I meditate on where that superhuman energy was flowing from, those spherical eyes alone come to my view. It is apparent to me that someone is working secretly behind the scenes. Sometimes situations take such a turn that I have to look for the one who is creating all these facilities and opportunities as if He is the auspicious soul doing all that," Gajapati went on as if he is watching a show with his half-open eyes and narrating the scene.

"I have crossed the southern boundary and marched further south many times. Often, I passed through enemy territory. While riding on horseback alone across a jungle and when the possibility of being caught by enemy forces lurked everywhere, I felt someone was giving me company. Can you guess who he could be, *Purohita* Mahapatra?"

Mahapatra had a brief answer, "No, Your Majesty, I can't."

"How is it that I experienced an unseen power accompanying me and gratified all my aspirations? Odisha's enchanting power is unique. Can it be of anyone other than Lord Jagannath? He resides in a huge chamber of my mind. Whichever path He shows, I follow without hesitation, not heeding anyone else. And the outcome had always been an inevitable victory."

"Many dignitaries of the kingdom call me lucky indeed. I am fortunate because that unseen power's supportive design catapulted me to the title of Gajapati from that of an industrious horseman, Raut. Has it ever been aforementioned in history?"

"No, Your Majesty, the occurrence of such an event was never known before," Mahapatra nodded in agreement.

"Do you think Mahapatra that an ordinary cavalryman can join the secret discussion with an aggressive Muslim ruler on behalf of His Majesty

Gangaraj Bhanudev? It so happened once that Bhanudev accepted me as his most trusted lieutenant. He gave me the overall military responsibility as chief of the cavalry force. What else would it be if this was not The Lord's blessing?

"I could never know how all my military operations in each campaign were smooth sailing. My accomplished army generals were bewildered by my achievement so precisely. All of us wondered who helped us unseen. Whether it be Sanskrit Mahabharata or Odia Mahabharata of Sarala Das, it is written in both that *Belalasena* witnessed the whole Mahabharata battle and perceived how one rotating wheel alone was manipulating the entire war. No confrontation was there. Correspondingly, all the victories were the covert blessings of Lord Jagannath. Even though no one is speaking out, all of us have experienced it. Two huge globular eyes were the guiding lights at the forefront of our military expedition.

"I never saw the weary figure of my Lord. I saw it in my last night's dream. It was not clear what he was absorbed in, but His face looked wan and drawn, eyes were lustreless as if he had travelled ten times the distance he does in *Sri Gundicha* car festival along the Broadway at Puri, and last is resting there to recoup. He hadn't a piece of golden ornament on His person then. I was trying to figure out why the Lord had come in such plainness, keeping all His decorations in the storehouse of jewellery. It must be the Car Festival.

There is no other festive occasion wherein He would be so much tired. But the Lord doesn't go on those occasions alone. Then, He is always in the company of His brother and sister. So what did I dream of where He had been?

"Tell me, *Purohita* Mahapatra, despite being the Gajapati, I'm unable to understand where is this long journey taking me. You are His servant, bound to Him in devotion. You alone can enlighten me as to why Jagannath is so sad. Why so much exhausted? The mystical smile on that enchanting ebony face of the Lord has vanished?" Gajapati, in this manner, was asking Mahapatra to interpret the meaning of that incomprehensible dream.

Before Mahapatra could answer, Gajapati continued non-stop, "The Lord was looking at me with His ever-altering eyes. His face was welling up with compassion. Why is He watching me with a sad face instead of pouring some of his grace to remove my distress? Has He indeed rushed to Kondapalli to see the construction of His temple? No, had He come for it, He would have come joyfully with His brother and sister. He would have expressed his happiness at the construction site.

Something needs to be clarified to me, Mahapatra. Jagannath has come from a long distance alone. I am unable to take it anymore. Unquestionably, He hasn't come running to us. There is a cause for this. From a secret understanding between me and the Lord, I left

Odisha. But here I am, stuck in a lonely desert-like place as if I'm in exile. Because of that confidential matter, Odisha has forgotten all my achievements in my action-packed life and asked me to explain my actions.

Since you are intimately involved in Jagannath rituals at Puri, Mahapatra, you are acquainted with His daily life. Can He feel the urge to leave the temple and run to Kondapalli? But He knows this Kapilendra is His Raut, His refugee. Kapilendra has never ignored His words. He felt he never violated Lord's farsighted decisions, although the five-year family feuds cut me like a whip. No matter if I rot on this throne till my last breath. He alone has chosen my successor; society has made me weary and helpless. It has put hurdles in my way. Does the cry of my suffering reach the Lord of Lords?" "Tell me, has the Lord come to us?" Elderly Gajapati was looking at Mahapatra with a humble and entreating gesture.

Mahapatra thought momentarily and said, "He is giving priority to Your Majesty because He is your own. Rarely does He reveal His intention to the head servant in a dream. If He appeared in your dreams, please give me the details to analyze and understand His message."

Gajapati said, "Sri Jagannath came to my dream and gave some indication. But He looked very much preoccupied and worried. The rest of the house where He found me is Vijayabahuda's resting place. I saluted

Him but couldn't see that loving smile on His lips. My soul shivered in utter gloom.

The Lord might have looked at me in such a way as to express His dissatisfaction over the commotion and noise of the enemy on our borders. But no, it's something else. Strange that the cause of Jagannath's measureless sorrow remains obscure to me! Is it a forewarning of some terrible disaster to happen?

In my life, once only I disobeyed Him, for which today I regret. It was when I was pressing deep into the South in a series of victories. Exactly then, the Lord instructed me to march towards Bengal, crossing the northeastern riverside of Ganga. Nowadays, when I see the resurgence of the enemy in our occupied region of Pannar, our campaigns deep into the South will be our nemesis. Coupled with this, our recent adversity in Mandaran Fort hints at insufficient alertness for our northern border. Success came to us when we fought with Bahamani, Malwa, Jaunpur and other Muslim rulers. Bengal would have been free from Muslim control if it repeated on the north boundary. Had Bengal been annexed into Odisha, the Odisha border would have been intact for a long time.

The Lord's heart escalated in sorrow when my mind faced such a dilemma. I felt he had taken a vow not to give any suggestions. I prostrated before Him and begged to be pardoned and also requested him to let him share his sorrow with me.

"So much sadness in that beautiful ebony face! What could be the reason?

"The Lord has no faith in the material world, no interest in wealth, family and landed property. But He has been down with so much sorrow that He left Jagannath temple to hasten to faraway Vijayabahuda. All these are undoubtedly unprecedented.

"I thought ornaments on my person don't fit well when my Lord is sad. I am equally painful. These ornaments on me are meaningless. I shall dedicate them to my Lord. But now that it is impossible here, my six Mahapatras will carry them to Him and deposit them in Jagannath temple.

"Oh! What nonsense am I thinking about? Can't I offer them myself that l shall entrust Mahapatras to do it?

"Suddenly, my dream ceased as if something blasted it into pieces. I couldn't believe my own experience. I failed to understand where my identity melted in the drive. The Lord alone knows why He distanced himself from me in the dream. I have a feeling of being in danger. Where has my identity gone? Despite my enormous cavalry force, why should I not donate my ornaments to the Jagannath temple instead of sending them by Mahapatras?

"The Lord just returned empty-handed.

"This strange dream has drawn my mind into

pitch darkness. Indeed, some evil is going to happen. That could be understood from The Lord's dejection. Well, what could that evil be? What danger is there in store for me tomorrow? I don't care a fig if my life is in peril. But I won't allow anyone to occupy even an inch of land from Odisha territory.

"The dream occurred again, and I saw the Lord has not deserted me. He was waiting as before in my room.

"I asked Him, 'Lord, excuse me for my wrong actions. Please have mercy on me to tell me why you look sad, my Lord. I shall leave no stone unturned to redress it.'

The Lord stood speechless in an unusual manner. Overwhelmed with sorrow, the two spherical eyes of the Lord brimmed with tears. Why is the Lord of Lords in deep melancholy? What hardship has permeated our lives?

I woke up. I thought Jagannath Himself had come hastily to Gajapati. What danger is dangling on his head for which His appearance has been gloomy?

"Now that you heard everything, Mahapatra, decipher this dream to me."

Mahapatras were silent, their eyes flooding with tears.

Gajapati felt as if he was lost, "Where is this world headed? Where did this Gajapati's prowess go?

Warangal under Odisha

The situation today has made me a mere spectator. The Lord today is also silent for some unknown terror. *Purohita* Mahapatra was in deep sadness because he failed to penetrate its meaning.

"What can it be? Gajapati is in peril? None of them could make any head or tail of what mishap would happen. The Lord must reveal it in Gajapati's dream.

Purohita Mahapatra consoled Gajapati. He advised him to leave Kondapalli to stay at Vijayabahuda Fort. The Lord, according to the dream, is waiting only there.

Just Dakshineswar Kumar arrived. He came to take the dust from Gajapati's feet and put it on his forehead. He is bound for Kondavidu because there has been infiltration into Odisha. He wanted Grandpa's advice.

Gajapati said, "*Trutiya,* the third! my mind has been blocked. You discuss with *Sandhibigraha* to find a way and set out for Kondavidu immediately."

Purohita Mahapatra and other Mahapatras got ready and left for Vijayabahuda per Gajapati's wish.

Fort Vijayabahuda

Gajapati was resolute on his decision to depart from Kondapalli and make his way to Vijayabahuda Fort, a mere hour's journey, roughly ten miles away. His conviction stemmed from the belief that Lord Jagannath was awaiting his arrival there. Accompanied by his six Mahapatras, Gajapati promptly set off for Vijayabahuda.

Within the Gajapati's chamber at the Fort, a substantial scroll painting depicting Lord Jagannath adorned one of the walls. Vijayabahuda Fort held a special place in the hearts of the people of Odisha and was strategically located. Interestingly, the Fort itself was not garrisoned with military forces; instead, Odisha soldiers from nearby Kondapalli were responsible for its protection. The bustling town of Vijayabahuda was situated on the north bank of the River Krishna, and it stood guard against the neighbouring Vijayanagara kingdom.

The month of December or *Pausa* brought a winter

atmosphere, and the greenery along the riverbank added to the charm of the surroundings. The Fort was adorned with a magnificent flower garden in full bloom, casting a vibrant array of colours. However, amidst this beauty, there were no souls blessed with the sensibility to appreciate it. Neither poets nor philosophers were present to be enchanted by the aesthetic wonders around them. In a place where militarism, battles and conquests held sway, the value of beauty seemed to go unnoticed.

Today, Odisha Gajapati has surrendered to spirituality. He has no more desire for the conquest of kingdoms. If there is any desire, it is to dissolve himself at the lotus feet of Lord Sri Jagannath.

Gajapati is seeking within himself the Lord of Lords, that round-eyed Jagannath. In his dream, he saw Him present in the Fort. The Lord was looking at him with grief-laden eyes. But where is He? In which part of the fortress?

The Lord of Lords! He can turn a cavalryman into the world's most potent Gajapati. He appeared one day in a dream, and the shape of an elephant poured the anointing holy water from a golden pot to let him ascend the throne. With the same intent, He made him a lifelong victor against the enemy. Indeed, there's now some heavenly work here in the Fort for which he has left *Srimandira* of Puri and is present here!

Gajapati is looking for his Lord in each chamber.

Mahapatras looked on. At last, Gajapati shouted, "Mahapatra, Come, let's go to the temple once. Lord Jagannath is beckoning." He changed mood after a moment and went in and out of some more chambers. Feeling tired, he sat suddenly on a chair at last.

Gajapati's surprise arrival at Vijayabahuda made many army officials assemble there. Antaranga Mahapatra asked them not to leave because Gajapati was not well. Yesterday Gajapati stayed at Kondapalli. They came late for his audience. He explained that the discussion is possible only when his condition improves.

When Gajapati reached Vijayabahuda, his mind seemed unsteady; for some reason, it had lost its balance. Antaranga Mahapatra couldn't figure out why Gajapati felt discomfort in his territory. He has seen many pictures and statues of his rebel son Hamvira Dev throughout the citadel, showcasing the Gajapati dynasty's bravery. All the familiar people of that place are admirers of Hamvira Dev. They praise the heroism of Odia Paika soldiers but praise Hamvira Dev a hundred times more.

This vanquished Andhra region has been under Odisha for about twelve years. This region was also under Birabhadra Reddy's control, who had forcibly occupied Rajamahendry. Odisha expelled Reddy from Rajamahendry twenty-two years ago. He managed to stay at Kondavidu, but Odisha took an opportunity to settle it. Reddy was a baggage-carrying ruler under

Vijayanagara. When Vijayanagara shrank, his bad days began.

Before a few moments of rest on the chair were over, Gajapati opened his eyes, looking for someone everywhere. There was no sleep in them. With a single-minded insistence, he thought Lord Jagannath was in one of the rooms. His search, therefore, must be on.

There were only sixteen rooms in the Fort. A temple to the South of the Fort was in the river's direction. It was an ancient riverside temple. Previously, the presiding deity of Vijayabahuda had been installed here. Since Odisha occupied it, it built a new temple on the southern side of the existing temple and consecrated Jagannath in it. There was a large crowd of five to six-foot-tall flower plants, creating the illusion of humans on their feet. The temple gate is east-facing, and a wall to the South separates the Fort from the river bed. There is a path from the doorstep, which had been closed with a narrow wooden door. This door led to the river bed. One has to go twenty-two low steps down to reach the river's flow.

Gajapati, too, came out of the trance. He is now conscious of having called six Mahapatras here. Gajapati was sure Jagannath was somewhere inside the Fort. He told them, "Look, the Lord is here. The Lord is playing hide and seek with me. He sent me here from Kondapalli. Here also, He is hiding from me. "

All the six Mahapatras stood around Gajapati in a circle in the meeting hall and looked steadily at him.

"But Jagannath neither is saying anything nor is appearing before me. But I can see He has not put on whatever ornaments He owns. My body will be devoid of all the ornaments on me now. You six faithful Mahapatras will offer all these at my Lord's feet and convey my last prayer, 'Your Raut, Kapila takes leave of You surrendering his last belongings."

Mahapatras was startled. What is all this Gajapati blabbering? He is well; He has complete devotion to Lord Jagannath. He can see Him by his supernatural insight. Why, then, is He giving hints of death?

"My Lord, you hear me from behind the door, looking at me also. Tarry, a while; let me see your majestic face to my heart's content. My end has come. You know it. Your raut named Kapila is going to shed this mortal body. While seated on the throne, you couldn't bear the travesty of truth like this. Hence, you have hurried here to give me your last darshan," Gajapati spoke, with his eyes fixed on the eastern door of the meeting hall.

Gajapati sprang up. He shouted toward the eastern door, "Please wait a moment, Lord, let me see your majestic visage. No hiding from me, please; my soul won't leave this body without your darshan."

Mahapatras could then surmise the meaning of those mysterious events. Gajapati was delirious when the end was coming. His lifelong presiding deity, his only protector, is before his insightful vision. He has come running to the Krishna river bank, only fixing his eyes on Him. The pure truth of his life is finding words in his lips. He is surrendering all his ornaments to the Lord. He has turned away from material wealth. The end is probably surrounding the Fort. It's Tuesday night; next will be Wednesday dawn.

As Gajapati Kapilendra Deva's life neared its end, his voice trembled with emotion as he called out, "Appear to me, Lord! You have come a long way in haste to see your humble servant. Why not reveal yourself to me now? Why do you hide from me in this moment? My breaths are numbered, and my senses are fading. Is there any strength left in my senses to bear the wondrous gaze of your eyes? I beseech you, Lord, manifest yourself before me. Let me behold you until you satisfy my soul in this final hour. I shall carry my body, which is truly your, and my soul, which is truly your shadow."

Gajapati's strength had waned, and could no longer rise. This was the same Gajapati who, for the last thirty-four years of his life, had ridden swiftly on horseback across the borders of Odisha in all directions. Now, he couldn't even take a few steps from the meeting hall to the eastern doorstep.

Invisible footsteps seemed to approach Gajapati, as if someone were hurrying to his side. He felt the presence of his Lord in his heart. "I am blessed, Lord,

Lord Jagannath

truly blessed," were Gajapati's final words, echoing in the sombre atmosphere. He bowed with folded hands. The greatest devotee of Sri Jagannath in the world at that time had finally departed from this life, resting eternally.

He was no longer there to serve Lord Jagannath as His devoted disciple the greatest "Rauta", but his senses had remained intact until the end, allowing him to feel the presence of his beloved deity, Lord Jagannath. His material body proclaimed, "My Lord, I have never strayed from your guidance!"

Cowards may experience many deaths before their final demise, but the valiant taste death only once!

A heavy silence descended upon the Mahapatras, and their grief erupted in loud lamentations.

It was Wednesday evening in the month of *Magha, Sakabda* 1388, which corresponds to February 1467 in the Gregorian calendar.

In the stormy sky above *Nila Chakra* flag of Lord Jagannath temple in Puri seemed to shine brighter, as one more star devotee was added to the celestial galaxy.

Odishan sculpture

Reincarnation of Odisha: Most Promising Moments

The annals of Odisha history are replete with moments of resilience, transformation, and resurgence. One such transformative phase began with the end of the Keshari dynasty and the rise of Chodaganga Deva from the Ganga dynasty. Chodaganga Deva's victory over Subarna Keshari marked the beginning of the Ganga dynasty's rule over Odisha, a dynasty that would hold sway for a remarkable 320 years. During this extensive reign, while the Ganga dynasty made significant contributions in various domains. Hindu kingdoms across Bharatavarsa were facing relentless treats from Muslim invaders, leading to the erosion of several Hindu territories.

Odisha's boundaries during the Ganga dynasty's rule mirrored the grandeur of ancient Kalinga in the first century B.C., stretching from the Ganges to the Godavari, and from the Kalinga Sea to Amarakantak. Ganga kings like Chodaganga Deva and Narasimha

Deva immortalised themselves through monumental temple constructions. Chodaganga Deva built the iconic temple at Puri, while Narasimha Deva's legacy is forever linked with the majestic Konark Sun Temple. Narasimha Deva distinguished himself not only through the defence of his kingdom but also through his bold military offensive, capturing territories and expanding Odisha's influence.

However, as the Ganga dynasty reign progressed, the threat from Afghan rulers, who had established themselves in Bengal, loomed large. These Afghan rulers periodically invaded Odisha, posing a significant challenge to the Ganga kings. The focus of Odisha's rulers was to safeguard the Jagannath Temple, a sacred institution central to Odia culture. The temple's idol was revered as living deities, and the Ganga kings ensured the temple's protection and continued celebration.

By installing Lord Jagannath, on the advice of religious teachers like Adi-Sankaracarya and Ramanuja, and by celebrating the day-to-day activities of the Lord as a living entity, they had swarmed the whole of Bharatavarsha with the fragrance of Hindu tradition. Jagannath Temple was the point of attraction for the Afghan invaders. They smashed idols and robbed jewellery stored in vaults. Rulers of Odisha have considered securing the Jagannath temple from falling into the hands of the Afghans as their primary duty.

If there was the slightest deviation in the arrangement of administrative power, rebel forces, both internal and external, were up in arms. One such incident occurred in the closing years of Ganga rule. It is said that when the end nears for a royal dynasty, a feeble successor is born – a leader with deranged psyche who cannot rise to the challenges of the time and fades into obscurity. This administrative and military inconsistency happened when the last Ganga king was on the throne.

The last Ganga king proved to be a weak and ineffective ruler, often depicted metaphorically as "*Matta*" or mad, and "kajjal" or a small black bird, symbolising selfishness. History remembes him as "Nisanka Bhanudev", a title that sarcastically alludes to his fearlessness born out of apathy. During his reign, Odisha southern territories, including Rajamahendry on the banks o f the Godavari and Kalinga Dandapat along the coast up to Visakhapatana, were lost. The Reddy ruler posed a constant threat to Odisha's borders. There was also the fear of the Reddy ruler encroaching further.

How can the northern border of the empire be peaceful in this situation? Afghan administrator, usurper of Banga, the Yavana or king of low caste people as Hindus took Muslims to be, were eager to attack Odisha, awaiting an opportunity to lightning strike on Odisha and loot the jewel-filled treasury of Jagannath temple. Thus Odisha attracted the Muslim ruler of Banga and the independent Muslim ruler of Jaunpur in the north. To acquire Odisha or to capture its black elephant, Jaunpur Nawab repeatedly taunted Odisha for war.

This Ganga king was indeed an outright failure in performing royal duties. Yet, he camped at Simadri fort or at Gudari Katak for months to re-acquire the southern border of Odisha and thus was carrying on a cold war against the Reddy ruler.

At this time, in the political firmament of Odisha, there was an ominous ring of zero energy, as if Odisha was hollow inside. For this reason, Banga and Jaunpur in the north, Reddy and Vijayanagara in the South, and Bahamani and Malwa in the west were putting pressure to possess the capital Bidanasi Cuttack. Advisors and administrators sought a strong general who could rescue the kingdom from is dire predicament.

In this critical moment, a radiant sun appeared on the political horizon of Odisha – a hero among heroes. He filled the frozen blood of *Odia Paika* soldiers with boundless warmth. Rejuvenation in Odisha with youthful greenery was evident. The heat of this sun was so enormous that it spilt beyond its bounds. Due to the most successful application of unimaginable force and skill, the soil of Odisha became worthy of the saying, "None but the brave deserves the earth." Here blew the eternal vernal air, the kingdom turned into 'Odisha Rashtra'; our language became Odia language'; and our State deity was 'Lord Jagannath', and we have the Gajapati gold coin, the Pagoda. Our poets and wise men enriched the Odia language with the 'Sarala Mahabharata' epic; Odishi dance scenes adorned the *Natyamandapa* of Jagannath Temple; it reverberated with Jayadev's Gita-Govinda, the Trinity of deities dazzled in gems and jewellery, and Odisha glittered with myriads of rituals and festivities.

Who was this hero of heroes? He was Suryavamsi or of the Surya dynasty, Gajapati *Maudamani Sri Sri Sri Gajapati Gaudeswar-Navakoti-Karnata-Kalabargeswar-Veeradhiveerabara-Kapilendra Devaa* (Gajapati - a king with an army of elephants;

Gaudeswar - the Lord of Bengal or Gauda, Nava-koti – the owner of nine Forts, Karnata-Kalabargeswar - the ruler of Karnataka region of Vijayanagara and Gulbarga of Telangana). His coronation took place on 29 June 1435 on a Monday at *Kruttibash Temple*, Bhubaneswar, which is also the beginning of *Kapilabda* or the regal era of Kapilendra Deva - Saka 1357; death - February 1467 in the month of Magha on the bank of Krishna, at Vijaya Bahuda (Vijayawada at present.)

Sri Jagannath is the Lord and ruler of Odisha, and Gajapati is his servant and caretaker. The Lord appeared in his dream and gave a command that was the blessing of God for Gajapati. This divine decree is inviolable. A similar revelation in a plan forced Gajapati to supersede his eldest son in matters of accession to the throne in favour of a younger son. This step later filled his last days with immeasurable tragedy. The eldest son distanced himself, and top generals became unruly. With a heavy distressing heart, he set out to defend the southern border accompanied by six of his *Mahapatras*, the ministers.

In face of mounting challenges and a divided royal family, Gajapati Kapilendra Deva set out to defend the southern border, accompanied by his loyal ministers. Tragically, he encountered a deathtrap awaiting him on the banks of the Krishna River. He offered all his ornaments to Lord Jagannath and departed for his heavenly abode.

Lord Jagannath

In the annals of Odisha's heroes, Kapilendra Deva stands second only to Kharavela. His unwavering dedication to the motherland and his unmatched love for Odisha are evident in his life's work. His reign rekindled the spirit of Odisha, breathing new life into the land. It was a time of great cultural and social resurgence, with the fragrance of Hindu tradition permeating Bharatavarsha. Kapilendra Deva's era witnessed the creation of masterpieces like the "Sarala Mahabharata," the enchanting Odissi dance in the *Natyamandapa* of the Jagannath Temple and the brilliance of Jayadev's "Gita-Govinda." The Trinity of deities in the Jagannath Temple dazzled with resplendent gems and jewellery, and Odisha shone with a multitude of rituals and festivities.

Gajapati Kapilendra Deva's legacy endures as a beacon of hope and resilience, a hero who emerged when Odisha needed him most. It is unlikely that Odisha will ever see another leader of his calibre and dedication.

Pranipata: Great Gajapati

Publisher's Note

Gajapati Kapilendra Deva was the Emperor of Odisha and established the Gajapati dynasty, Gajapati denoting the "master of elephants." Really in fifteenth century India, military power was vested on frontline mastodon forces as the forward movers in days when canons were not discovered to be used. Dr. Indramani Jena's historical fiction novel brings to light premier Gajapati achievements emphasizing the military power and people oriented administration that characterised his era.

The novel aims to shed light on this forgotten emperor and his contributions to Indian history while blending historical accuracy with a compelling narrative about his life. The note also underscores the lasting cultural impact of Gajapati Kapilendra Deva such as every baby born in Odisha since Kapilendra's time has the birth almanac, *Jataka* written on a palm leaf starting with the title of the Gajapati.

This historical novel promises to offer the readers

a unique perspective on Gajapati Kapilendra Deva's life and times, bringing an often-overlooked historical figure back into the spotlight. It's a testament to the enduring legacy of this remarkable ruler and his significance in the history of India.

The publisher's note provides further insights into the author's unique approach in crafting this historical novel about Gajapati Kapilendra Deva. The author's background in writing novels that blend elements of fantasy and mysticism is highlighted, particularly in his previous work, "Salabhanjika," which delves into the life of Emperor Kharavela.

In this historical novel, the focus in on the last two months of Gajapati Kapilendra Deva's life, emphasizing the themes of grief, sorrow and devotion. The author's portrayal of the Gajapati's unwavering commitment to Lord Jagannath's dream, even in the face of impracticality and societal challenges, is a central element of the narrative.

The author's research process is mentioned, which includes a through analysis of available historical evidence, rituals, temple facts, inscriptions, and publications. Additionally, the author incorporates legendary quotations attributed to Gajapati Kapilendra Deva, adding depth to the portrayal of this historical figure.

Readers are encouraged to explore this novel as it offers a glimpse into an era that existed eight centuries ago, encompassing various aspects of society, polity, warfare, religion, and the spirit of the people.

The note concludes by mentioning the availability of the book on platforms like Global Amazon, Flipkart and Black Eagle Intellect Centre, making it accessible to wider audience interested in historical fiction.

Pranipata: Assets of Great Kapilendra

References:

❖ Mahatab, Harekrushna.(1964).*Odisha Itihas*. Binaribag, Cuttack-2: Dr. Harekrushna Mahatab Foundation.

❖ Mukherjee, Prabhat Kumar. (1981).*History of Gajapati Kings of Orissa*, KitabMahal.

❖ Sahu,Nabil Kumar.(1974).*JatiraItihas*.

❖ Banerjee,R.D.(1930),reprinted 2016. *History of Orissa*, New Delhi: Abhijit Publications.

❖ Rao, C.V.Ramachandra.(1988).*The Suryavansh Gajapatis of Kalingotkal Political History.* Nellore: Manas Publications.

❖ Kulke Herman. *Kshatriaization and social change: A Study in Orissa Setting*.

❖ Mishra, Patitapabana.(2016).*Eastern Ganga and Gajapati Empire, Cyclopedia of Empires*.

❖ Bhuyan, Annapurna. (1999). *Kapilendra Deva o tankasa-sanakala*. Utkal Viswavidyalaya.

❖ Subramanyam,R.(1957).*Suryavanshi Gajapati*. Waltaire: Andhra Viswavidyalaya.

- Sahu,K.C. *Madhyajugiyajivanasaili o bhashasanskruti.*

- Panda,Sisir Kumar. *Medieval Orissa's A Socio-economic Study.* Delhi:Mittal Publications

- Pattanayak,Mahendra.(1947).*Utkal Pratibha (Gajapati Kapilendra Deva).* Berhampur: Students Store.

- Mahapatra,Godavarish.(1959).*Amara Charitamala.* Berhampur: New Students Store.

- Rajaguru, S. N.(1960).*Inscriptions of Odisha. Bhubaneswar.*

- Acharya Srinibas. *Gajapati Kapilendra Deva.* Srikshetra-Srijagannath Srigajapati.

- Manshingh, Mayadhara. *PrabuJagannathanka Desharapratha*

- Tripathy, Kunjabihari. (2021). *Odia bhasa O Lipira Udbhaba* Utkal Vishwabidyalaya

- Sahu, Bijaya Ketana. *Sunabesara Prakruta Itihasa.*

- Mishra,Purnachandra. (2013). *Mahari System.*

- *Madala Panji*

- *Sarala Mahabharata*

- Internet data, Wikipedia. *Gajapati Samrajya, Kapilendra Deva, Odisha Vijayanagara Satabarsia Juddha*

- Copper plate and stone inscriptions (Bhubaneswar Lingraj temple, Puri Jagannath temple, Paga Gopinathpur Jagannath temple, Raghudevpur, Rajamahendry, Vellaganani, Srirangam Temple, Waltaire etc.

Black Eagle Books

www.blackeaglebooks.org
info@blackeaglebooks.org

Black Eagle Books, an independent publisher, was founded
as a nonprofit organization in April, 2019. It is our mission
to connect and engage the Indian diaspora and the world at
large with the best of works of world literature published
on a collaborative platform, with special emphasis on
foregrounding Contemporary Classics and New Writing.